THE WALLS THAT DIVIDE

(CITY ON THE SEA SERIES BOOK 2)

HEATHER CARSON

All Rights Reserved.

Copyright © 2021 Heather Carson

Courtesy of Blue Tuesday Books

Cover Design by Fay Lane at faylane.com

ISBN: 9798702916330

☦ CHAPTER ONE ☦

The wind turns cold. It dances across my bare shoulders as I retrieve my sandals from the base of the cliff. The shoes lay where I left them, but the air doesn't feel the way it did just a few hours ago.

Wisps of fog come from over the sea, reaching its arm towards our city and tapping against the wall that blocks us from the earth. I've never known fog to roll in like this. Drips of moisture run down my back and wet my hair. It's a bad omen.

I wrap my arms around my body as I head to the docks. My gaze is focused on the planks in front of me. Nothing is right anymore. I know this now. Our world is a lie, but this feels different than that. Something awful is about to happen.

I promised myself I wouldn't look. My father's machine should be gone by now. Torn and gutted, piece after piece, by the watchmen who say they're here to protect us. All that work for nothing. My father's life is over.

The mist wraps around me as it continues its assault against the wall. It's teasing me, telling me that I need to see it. As much as it pains me, I turn my head slightly. One final look to say good-bye.

Part of the machine still stands. The watchmen have abandoned their work. Their solid faces trained for watching are staring intently at the sea. They don't notice me watching them. *Ironic, isn't it?*

A bitter chuckle blows hot air through my nose as I step cautiously onto the jagged rocks. Calder said if I didn't cause any trouble that they would leave me alone, but I can't stop myself from seeing what's more important than dissembling the device that was supposed to save the earth.

Whatever it is has them frozen to the spot. With tense muscles and bulging eyes, they stare down at the sea beneath them. Like seagulls trained on a child eating, they don't dare move. They're so preoccupied with whatever is happening on the rocks below the cliff they don't notice as I walk up behind them. I balance on the ledge and peer over to see what they are seeing.

A weak cry escapes my lips. The *Hronn* has crashed into the rocks. Her bow is up like she tried to climb them before breaking in half. The water pushes her closer to the shore as if the sea is willing her to go home. There's a watchman in the tide wading closer to the wreckage. He looks up and his eyes meet mine. *Calder.*

He lowers his face and dives beneath the waves. I clap my hand over my mouth to stop myself from screaming. Tordon's younger brother Endre is in there. A memory of his gentle smile flashes across my mind as I remember him following Tordon everywhere as a child. He has to be okay.

"You shouldn't be here." Drake puts his hand on my shoulder and my eyes fixate on the curve of his knuckles. I fight back revulsion as I shrug them off my skin. The watchmen turn their attention to me. Although Calder's warning is still fresh in my mind, there's no physical way I could walk away from this until I know that Endre is alright.

"Please," I beg conjuring up the politeness that came so easily to me a week ago. "I know him. I know his family. I just need to see if he's okay."

Drake blinks. There's no sympathy in him, but there's something about my voice that makes him hesitate for a moment.

"Let's go," he says pulling me by my arm away from the sea.

But he's too late.

Calder emerges from the twisted carcass of the *Hronn* with Endre's body in his arms. I struggle to breathe. Endre's face is blue. Weak blue, the color of the winter sky. His hand that spills from the side of his body drags limply in the pull of the water. Around his neck is a rope. It cuts deeply into the pale skin. I take in this all as detailed fragments, focusing on the truth in front of my eyes, and force myself to see it.

Calder looks up again and his eyes lock with mine. Fear, disdain, sympathy- I don't know what his face shows and I couldn't care less what he feels right now. My heart breaks as I watch my friend's dead brother being carried in a watchman's arms.

Drake tugs at me again. I can't imagine that I was too heavy to move the first time, but maybe the horror of it all has turn me into stone.

"You need to leave now," he commands.

I struggle to find my voice. "I need to tell his family what happened."

Drake looks back over his shoulder. The older watchmen nod. The silence in their communication is unsettling.

"Okay," he says softly. "Tell them we are handling this. We'll bring the body to his house."

"Endre." I stare hard into his startled eyes. "The body's name is Endre. He's the second son of Aegir and one of the sweetest kids I know."

"Okay," Drake says. I glance back down at Calder. He has Endre's body on the small strip of beach that the low tide exposes. He turns it over gently, inspecting the state of decay. More watchmen climb down to help him.

Drake presses a finger against my chin making me face him once more. "Go tell his family that we will bring Endre home."

*

I shiver against the fog. While I was up on the cliff, I lost track of time and with the sky this shade of gray it's hard to tell what part of the day it is. I go to the docks first to see if Aegir's fishing fleet has returned.

All the boats are nestled into the harbor and tied down for the night. Aegir and Tordon will be home by now. This means I've missed my shift for the spinners. I'm sure I'll be reprimanded tomorrow, but none of that seems to matter anymore. I have to get to Tordon's house. They need to hear this from me, not from the cold and careless lips of the watchmen.

The wharf is silent as the owners close up their shops. With the fog wrapping around our city, there's no customers out this evening. I pass down the main walkway heading deeper into the maze of planks toward the docks where the houses sit. Some are propped up on rocks and some balance precariously on beams built over the sea.

Further out are the ones that float. Tiny houses tethered to the end of the city wharfs and worn down by each passing storm. My mother used to threaten me and my sister that we would have to live in one someday because we were useless and no one wanted us. Thankfully, I don't have to go to them today.

Tordon's house sits closest to the wall. With Aegir's fishing fleet and his brewing side business, he earns enough for one of the safest and largest houses in the city.

I play with words in my head as I walk. Condolences and sympathies, anything to soften the blow that is to come. Yet nothing sticks firmly in my mind. There is no phrase to ease the pain of this news. It just has to be me that brings it.

Even so, I hesitate at the door. The noise within is filled with lightness. There are pans moving in the kitchen and deep chested laughter as the boys tease each other inside these walls. I don't want to be the one to ruin this. My hand falls back to my side before it gets a chance to knock. Maybe it would be better if the watchmen came. They probably know what to say. Who am I but some stupid girl who couldn't even tell Tordon it was weird to kiss him and I didn't want to try it again?

But the words Tordon spoke yesterday whisper in my ear, pushing me forward to the door. *It's like you finally found your voice.* I bite my lip and raise my hand once more to knock. If I really found it, then it's time to use it to help the ones I love.

*

"Hey Brooke." Tordon's smile fades as he sees my face. He opens the front door wide. "What's wrong?" I take deep breaths and force myself not to cry.

"Is that our little Brooke?" Aegir's deep voice bellows from the kitchen. "Bring her in son. Dinner is almost ready. She can eat with us."

Tordon looks helplessly at his father and then to me. I nod reassuringly and step into their home. My hand slips into Tordon's hand. He tenses at the touch. It seems like a lifetime ago that we held hands easily. If we've never tried to kiss, maybe we'd still maintain that innocent connection. Maybe not, but at least we are still friends. I shake my head to clear the thoughts. Now isn't the time to dwell on this.

"I'm glad you came." The giant stands bare chested as grease from the stove pops against his skin. Aegir glances down at my hand still intertwined with Tordon's and pretends not to notice, but he can't hide the happiness that lights up his blue eyes. "It's been too long, but never mind that now. Everything is better tonight."

"Actually." I squeeze Tordon's hand tightly in my own. "There's something you need to know."

Tordon's youngest brother Beirger sits at the table. His attention is focused on me. With wind burnt cheeks and glossy eyes, I can tell he's had a hard day fishing.

"Maybe you should go to the other room." I smile at the boy.

"Is this about our conversation earlier?" Tordon asks quietly. I shake my head as I motion to Beirger.

"I'm big enough to listen." The boy stubbornly refuses to leave.

"It's Endre, isn't it?" Aegir's voice is suddenly hoarse. The spatula clatters carelessly to the floor.

People break in different ways. Sometimes it's a slow crack. Like the way Tordon tightens his grip on my hand crushing the bones in my fingers. The muscles in his jaw flex as he clenches his teeth. The anger and adrenaline passes down his arm into my palm. He says nothing. It terrifies me.

More so than Beirger's blank stare. He's not old enough to understand what is happening. I kick myself for answering in his presence. But sometimes people are like this, silently processing the pain and storing it away to come back to later. Who am I to judge his reaction? He fiddles with the seal skin sail he was repairing. His chubby fingers tug at the tanned material sprawled out on the kitchen table. I'm hopeful that he hasn't even heard what I just said. Maybe he'll come back and deal with it when he's older.

Sometimes people shatter. Like the thin ice we get in the coldest part of winter which splinters into fragments of cracked water. Like a broken ship crashing against the rocks. Like Endre's boat. Aegir crumples into a heap onto the kitchen floor.

"Not my son!" he screams through breaking sounds that wrench from his chest. "They can't have my baby boy."

Tordon grips my hand tighter as his father curses the gods. Aegir's shrieks of a heartbroken man are loud enough to wake the dead. Their pain washes over me in waves, but I can't let myself feel it. They need me to be strong for them now, or maybe I need me to be strong. Whatever it is, we'll figure it out together.

"Come sit down," I plead with Tordon prying his vice like fingers from my hand. He's lost in a silent world of agony but his body obeys my request. I move into the kitchen and blow out the flame on the stove. Simple tasks they shouldn't have to worry about.

"Are you hungry?" I ask Beirger who sits staring at his hands.

"Not right now. I'll eat later. I think I want to go lay down." He leaves the room without glancing back at his father or eldest brother.

Aegir's sobs rock his heavy body. His head rests on top of his arms. I move the food away from the heat and sit on the floor beside him.

"I'm so sorry," I say leaning my shoulder against him to provide comfort. The words sound as shallow to me as they did when spoken by well-wishers after my father passed. I try again, finding the truest words I can. "This shouldn't have happened. Endre was a good sailor. You did everything in your power to make sure of that."

"It wasn't enough." Aegir's voice cracks. I use my thumbs to wipe the tears from his eyes and like a child he lets me. The sight of this great big broken man tears at my heart. He's never looked so small before.

"The watchmen will be here soon," I remind him. "Why don't we get you to the table so you can sit?"

He nods despondently. It takes every bit of strength I have to pull him to his feet and lead him to the head of the table. He falls heavily onto his seat beside Tordon. Aegir glances at the empty chair where Endre normally sits and a fresh wave of tears streams down his face. Tordon stands and kicks back his chair sending it sliding into the wall.

I reach out to him just as the watchmen knock on the door. He turns his back to his father and begins to shake as the built-up anger consumes him. The watchmen knock again. I leave the men to their grief as I rush to open the door.

Calder's face is the first one I see. His eyes light up in recognition but there's a stoic hardness to his features. The other three watchmen mirror his expression as they carry the body wrapped in plastic into the house. A fifth watchman follows them inside.

There are no markings on their uniforms. There never has been, but with the way the last watchman carries himself it's easy to tell that he's in charge. He's tall and skinny with graying hair and a crooked nose that looks as if it didn't heal straight after a few too many fights. But there's a gentleness in the way he moves that doesn't match his air of superiority. Something about him seems familiar, but I can't seem to place it right now.

"Oh gods," Aegir's heartbroken cry rings throughout the room. "How did this happen?"

The watchmen place Endre on the kitchen table. Beirger's face blanches as he stares at the body from the crack of his open bedroom door. He quickly slams it shut when Aegir begins to unwrap his son.

Aegir stifles his cries and replaces them with a soothing hum. I instantly recognize the tune. It's one of the sailing songs that the fishermen sing out on the boats. Except there are no vulgar words and he quiets the melody into a lullaby. It's something one would sing to a newborn baby.

A song that Tordon must know well because at the sound of his father's voice, his eyes well with tears. I slip quietly behind the watchmen to stand by his side and wrap my arm around his back. This time he doesn't tense but relaxes just enough to let me know this is where I'm needed.

Aegir exposes Endre's head and rests his chin next to his face. The white whiskers of his beard brush against Endre's forehead as he continues to sing.

The rope around Endre's neck is gone. There's a faint outline from where it was, but it's almost unnoticeable unless you thought to look. I glance up from the body to study Calder's reaction. His head is lowered in respect.

It's the tall watchman who came in last that begins to speak, "We are sorry for your loss, Aegir. He was a good man."

Aegir says nothing as he hums to soothe the dead child in his arms.

"Do you know what happened?" Tordon asks through gritted teeth.

"No, son, we don't," the man replies. "There were no witnesses. No signs of foul play. The boat is being towed to the wrecking yard. You're welcome to take a look, but there was nothing out of the ordinary." Tordon tenses but remains silent.

My jaw drops. "Then how do you explain..." The watchmen turn as one unit to look at me. My voice falters. I inhale deeply to get the courage to demand more answers.

"Thank you, Henry." Aegir wipes the tears from his eyes. "We'll take it from here."

The tall watchman, Henry, nods and turns on his heel to leave. The other four follow him out the door and close it gently behind them. Aegir resumes his lullaby once they are gone. Tordon angrily clenches and unclenches his fist as he stares at his brother's feet.

I need to tell them about the rope. The watchman's clear omission of that detail is wrong. But they are in so much pain that I hesitate. Is telling them something on pure speculation only going to make their suffering worse? Maybe the watchman was right to leave it out. It would only make them wonder what they could've done to stop it or make them angry enough to try and avenge his death. Still, don't they have a right to the truth? Don't we all have a right to the truth?

"Can you check on Beirger for me, Brooke?" Aegir sighs heavily as the weight of grief crushes his chest.

Each passing minute throughout the night brings me further away from mentioning the rope. I coax Bierger into eating and sit with the boy until he falls asleep. Tordon leaves in the early morning to ready the boat for the burial at sea. Aegir asks me to stay. We manage to get the plastic off and roll Endre in his blankets.

"It never gets easier to lose someone you love," Aegir says heavily. He smooths down the hair on Endre's head. I don't think he is really speaking to me so I just sit in silence next to him.

It's early dawn when Tordon returns. Aegir lifts Endre in his arms and cradles him like a child as he carries him through the city.

The fishermen on the docks are silent. They remove their caps and lower their faces. Aegir climbs easily onto the *Bara* despite the burden he carries. Tordon lifts Beirger onto the bow and turns to reach for my hand.

The burial is usually a private one. I wasn't intending to get on the boat. Tordon senses my hesitation.

"I thought you'd want to be with your family right now." I smile reassuringly.

"You are our family, Brooke." He holds his hand out once more and this time I take it.

☦ CHAPTER TWO ☦

I was young when we buried my grandmother. My father forbid us to cry. Instead, we threw a little party on the boat while my mother sat sullenly below deck. It wasn't her mother that passed away. I never met that grandmother. My mother just hated being on boats. She hated a lot of things.

My father released his mother's body into the sea and we sat on the deck telling our favorite memories of her. Meghan had more memories than I did. She's older so it made sense, but I remember being jealous that they had more time with her. I never said that aloud though, I didn't want to ruin the happy time.

My father scratched letters into the door of our boat. *Remember.* Meghan figured out what it said long before I could sound it out. *"That's right."* Our father smiled. *"Always remember the good times."*

I sit silently now as Tordon and Aegir let go of Endre's body. It sinks beneath the waves and he is gone. There's no joy and laughter like there was for my grandmother. No sugar kelp treats and singing.

Aegir and Tordon stare quietly at the horizon. Beirger moves to take his place beside them.

I patiently watch their ceremony and pray to the gods it brings them some measure of comfort. We are so far out that I can't see the city behind us. There are miles and miles of endless sea, the ripples of the water reflecting the sun and shining it back to the sky. The boat rocks on the gentle waves. I scan the horizon looking for a familiar landmark, but I'm not sure I've ever been out this way.

"That's the offshore drillers." Tordon breaks his silence as he sees me trying to make out the gleam in the distance. At the sound of his son's voice, Aegir snaps out of his trance and straightens his shoulders.

"Is there anything you boys want to say?" His voice is rough from the night spent crying. Tordon and Beirger shake their heads. He turns to me hopefully, "Brooke?"

Instead of turning to the sea, I focus on their faces. "Do you remember the time Endre stole some of your beer to impress his friends?"

There it is. The slightest hint of a smile on their faces. It isn't much, but it's enough to know there's hope.

"I've never seen someone get that sick," Aegir chuckles softly.

"You didn't have much sympathy for him then." Tordon smiles. "You worked him hard the next day."

Beirger stares in amazement at the side of his brother he never saw.

"He was green." Aegir wipes a happy tear from his eye. "The sea was rough on him that day, as she should've been, but he never once complained. He took his punishment like a man and learned his lesson. It was easier to teach him than it was to teach you."

He ruffles the top of Tordon's head. Tordon doesn't push him away in embarrassment like he normally would.

"Endre might not have complained but he did spew chunks all over the dock as soon as we got back." Tordon gags as he remembers the stench of it. Aegir laughs softly before turning around the boat to take us back home.

*

"You need to get some sleep." Tordon looks at me with concern as I sway on the solid dock. "Let me walk you to the tavern."

"I'll be fine," I reassure him. "You need to stay with your father right now."

Aegir begins to remove crates from the boats. The remaining eight boats of his fishing fleet will get a deep cleaning today. Like most, he knows hard work is the only way to survive and right now he knows even harder work is the best way to survive the sadness. If it brings him comfort, I'm happy for it. But I do feel sympathy for everyone he will force to help.

"Okay." Tordon gives me a broken smile. "Thank you for everything. I don't know how we would've gotten through last night and this morning if it wasn't for you. I'm glad we're friends again."

"Me too." I hug him tightly. "Also, I've been thinking, when you go to check out the boat at the wrecking yard, I'd like to come with you."

"What makes you think I want to see it?" he asks.

"Because I know you." I stifle a yawn with the back of my hand.

"Alright," he says. "I'll come get you before I go. Now you go home and get some sleep."

*

As beautiful as the idea of sleep sounds, I don't go straight to my room above the tavern. Gertrude will want an immediate explanation of why I missed the morning shift. I'm not ready to tell her what happened, but that's not why I don't stop. There's something I've been putting off for too long and I know how worried she gets.

*

"Before you even start, I want to tell you how incredibly sorry I am." I close my sister's door behind me. Zander squeals in delight, spilling the contents of his breakfast bowl onto the table. Bits of broth-soaked seaweed cling from the side like they're trying to escape whatever concoction my sister mixed up.

"I'll take care of that," I laugh.

Meghan stares at me in disbelief as Thora coos in her arms. There are dark circles under her eyes and her hair is wild. Guilt smacks me in the face. She has enough on her plate with the new baby, she doesn't need me to add anymore. After burying Endre this morning, I swear I'm going to be a better sister from here on out.

"Thank the gods you're alright." Her bottom lip quivers. "We heard about the watchmen going to your room and then we couldn't find you yesterday. I was so worried you disappeared."

"I think I'm still here." I lift my arm to inspect it.

"Stop it," Megan giggles. "That isn't funny."

"It's kind of funny." I smile as I finish cleaning the breakfast mess.

"Are you going to tell me what happened?" Meghan wipes the tears from her eyes. "You might as well since you're still here."

"Go play in the back room," I tell Zander. He pouts and begins to protest, but a stern look from his mother sends him scurrying away.

"I don't know where to start," I sigh as I collapse onto the bench at the table. "Endre's boat crashed into the rocks. His dead body was inside. I spent the night at Aegir's with them. We buried him this morning."

"Oh, Brooke," she gasps. She settles Thora on the floor and gently sits beside me. "Poor Aegir. What can I do to help?"

"Nothing right now." I shake my head. "They'll be working all day."

"Maybe I should make them some food." Meghan looks to the kitchen.

I grip her hand in mine to stop her from this plan. "They might just need some time alone. Maybe it'll be better to send Rowan to check on them in a few days."

"Plus, there's more I need to tell you," I explain. "They took Jillian."

"Who took Jillian?" Meghan starts as her eyes open wide in surprise. "The watchmen? But why?"

"I think it has something to do with what happened to our father." My voice drops to a whisper and I glance back over my shoulder. The paper burns a hole in my pocket. I haven't taken it out since yesterday on the cliff. "Shane said a man came asking for plans to their growing system and she wanted to give them to him. Later that day the watchmen came and took her away."

"No." Her face pales. "That doesn't make any sense."

"But don't you see that it does?" I stare into her eyes, willing her to understand. "They wanted the plans to dad's machine this whole time. That's why they were watching me. That's why they went to my room. They took the plans he left and said they were dangerous."

"I told you we needed to get rid of them." Her tone is sharp. "Oh gods Brooke, what did you do?"

"I didn't do anything," I groan. "They took the plans and then they broke down the machine. They said I'm not being watched anymore as long as I don't cause any problems."

"That's a relief," she cries. "At least we can finally put this all behind us and move on with our lives."

"Are you not hearing what I'm telling you?" I stare at her incredulously. "There's something wrong with the watchmen. They aren't being honest with us."

"No, you are not hearing what I am saying." She gives me the same look that caused Zander to hurry away. "You need to leave this alone. Forget it ever happened. Talking like this never does anyone any good. It will kill me if anything ever happens to you. I'm begging you to stop."

"What are you not telling me?" I try to read her face, but exhaustion causes my vision to blur.

"I'm telling you everything you need to hear." She rolls her eyes. "Don't go making problems out of thin air. You are not our mother."

"That's what I'm trying to explain," I cry. "I don't think she had anything to do with his disappearance."

"Dad didn't disappear," she states calmly. "He drowned."

"Really think about this," I beg. "He was a strong swimmer. How exactly would he have drowned? And the only person who saw it happen was a watchman. Sounds pretty suspicious, don't you think?"

"Enough." Meghan slaps her hand against the table. "I refuse to let you go down this path. You want to know who used to talk like this? Both of our parents. Look what good it did them."

"Why did you never tell me this?" I gasp. "Did dad not trust the watchman either?"

"I didn't tell you because I've always tried to protect you." She glares. "And it doesn't matter what he thought. One of our parents is bitter and crazy. The other one is dead. Neither is a fate I want for you."

"Don't you want to know what happened to him?" The emotional turmoil of the past few days makes my shoulders sag and my voice comes out with less conviction than I feel. "I need to know the truth."

"The truth won't change anything," Meghan scolds. "You've been given the chance to live a good life free from the watchman's eyes. Don't be stupid and mess this up."

"Fine," I sigh as I stand to leave. Calder's paper sits unseen in my pocket. If she has secrets then I can have them too. *I'll be a better sister another day.*

*

The lunch rush is already over by the time I enter the tavern. Gertrude is wiping down the bar counter. Zoe and Rupert laugh from behind the kitchen door. Every sound is heightened as I force my lead feet to move across the floor.

"There you are," Gertrude says. I look up expecting her to begin a lecture but there is only kindness on her face. "It's been a long night."

I nod slowly, too tired to formulate a response. Since she isn't being harsh about me missing work, I assume she already knows what happened. Word travels fast here.

"Be that as it may." She blinks to dry her eyes and chews the inside of her cheek. "You've already missed two mornings in a row. Go sleep for a few hours, but I'll need you to cover the night shift."

"The spinners," I start to say but she cuts me off.

"I already spoke with them. They understand."

I nod again and will my feet to continue moving to the metal staircase that leads to the rooms above the bar.

"Did you eat?" Gertrude calls after me.

"I'm alright," I mumble as I cling to the banister and practically crawl up the steps. The bed calls to me when I open the door. My eyes are already closed as I fall upon it and drift into an inky black escape.

*

There's a heavy knocking on my door that matches the pounding in my brain. It pulls me from the depths of unconsciousness and I groan as I force myself to sit up on the bed.

"Just a minute," I call in a voice cracked from sleep. The window in my room is open and the afternoon sun blinds me as soon as I open my eyes. I hurry to the wash basin and splash my face with water. My mural with the ship tossed around on the stormy sea stares back at me. There's so much blank space left to paint. I should be happy that I now have all the time in the world to fill it.

I remove the paper from the pocket in my dress just as the knocking begins again. Briefly I panic. *What if Calder is playing a trick on me and the watchmen are coming to take me away?* The knocking grows more insistent. I quickly slide the paper in the crevice between my mural and the wall as my heartbeat races inside my chest.

"Finally," Zoe sighs gently as I open the door. The hand she used to knock with gracefully retrieves the second plate of food that was balancing on her forearm. "Gertrude asked me to wake you up."

"Mommy, I'm hungry." Iris crosses her little arms over her chest and pouts from the open doorway of Zoe's room.

"Just a second honey." Zoe turns back to me. "Are you going to be alright?"

"I think so," I say. My stomach growls as the smell of food surrounds me. "Thanks for waking me up."

"Don't thank me just yet," Zoe laughs. "It looks like it's going to be a full house tonight. Hurry and get some food before you don't get another chance."

*

Rupert ladles a large helping of crab soup into a bowl and hands it to me with a smile. The tenderness that everyone is showing is a little unnerving. It was only a week ago that coming home meant dealing with my mother screaming and searching through empty cupboards for dried fish jerky. I force myself to ignore the guilt of blaming her for my father's death and instead try to be appreciative of what I have now. At least the food is good.

I hurry to finish just as the other girls arrive for the evening shift. The customers speak in hushed tones as they huddle over their plates. Most of them spent their day on the docks or out fishing so they've already seen Aegir. Their tips are generous tonight. The whole city must know what I did.

Cold sweat forms on the back of my neck as a group of watchmen arrive and climb the steps to their usual place in the loft. I scan their faces. Drake and Calder are here.

"Sarah will serve them tonight." Gertrude places a reassuring hand on my shoulder. "Why don't you take care of the tables in the front?"

"I'll be okay," I state while tucking my hair behind my ears.

She gives me a resigned shrug. "If that's what you want."

It isn't what I want at all. There is no rational part of me that wants to be climbing these steps right now and serving these jerks. But I know what I don't want. I don't want to let them win by making me scared enough to hide and I want answers. I inhale deeply as I enter the loft.

"What can I get you gentlemen tonight?" The room goes silent as they look at me. Calder's smug grin falters and the color drains from his face. *Good,* I think gaining a confidence I never knew I could have. *I hope I make you uncomfortable. Serves you right.*

Drake is the first to regain his smile. "I'll have a beer. And why don't you let me buy one for you too?"

"No thank you." I blink to hide the rage burning through my eyes and force myself to smile. "I would love that, but I'm working tonight. Maybe some other time."

"Well, how about beers for the rest of us then?" another watchman asks politely.

"Of course, sir. Whatever you need."

The other watchmen nod and return to their lighthearted conversations. All except Calder who stares past me at the wall in silence. I quickly take a head count before heading downstairs to place their order.

For the first time in months, my heart isn't pounding in my chest after interacting with the watchmen. *I don't want to be afraid anymore.* This realization taunts me. If I don't cause trouble then I won't have to be afraid. *But then I'd be living in a different kind of fear.* I absentmindedly place cups on the bar counter for Gertrude to fill. *And if I stay quiet, I'll never learn the truth.*

I barely notice the weight of the full tray in my arms until I'm no longer carrying it. The sudden lightness snaps me back to reality. Calder stands stone faced at the base of the stairs holding the tray in his hands.

"What are you doing?" he whispers harshly. "I told you to keep your head down."

"I'm doing my job." I glare at him. "Now get out of my way so I can work."

"This is dangerous." He squares his shoulders. "I refuse to be a part of this."

"No one is asking you to be a part of anything." I mirror his stance and we stare eye to eye. "Give me the tray and get out of my way."

"I shouldn't have given you the paper," he growls angrily. His comment catches me off guard and I turn to look over my shoulder, but no one can see us standing in the shadows of the staircase like we are.

"It was foolish," he continues. "You are reckless and can't be trusted."

"I can't be trusted?" I scoff. "What about you and all your lies?"

"I don't lie." He narrows his eyes. "There are some things you are better off not knowing."

"I think I can be the judge of that." I raise my chin. He thrusts the tray back into my arms and I fumble to keep the glasses from spilling. When I look back up, he is gone.

*

When I reach the top of the steps, Drake leans his long arms over the banister in the loft and scans the crowd below us. "Where'd our friend run off to?"

"No idea." I shrug.

He eyes me warily. "There's something about you that gets under his skin."

"I can't imagine what that is." I feign an innocent smile.

"It doesn't matter." Drake shakes his head and chuckles. "Is your friend Lena coming in tonight?"

"No." I push past him with the tray.

"Hey, wait up." He hurries to match my stride. "About the other night, that was just official business. You don't need to worry about it anymore. I want to make sure there are no hard feelings."

"None at all." I smile sweetly. The taste of sugar burns the back of my tongue like acid. "You were just doing your job."

☦ CHAPTER THREE ☦

I wanted to check on Tordon and Aegir after my shift, but my tired feet and pounding head protest against me leaving. Once I'm alone in my room, I use my fingernail to edge the paper from its hiding place behind the mural. I curl underneath my soft blankets and unfold the material to reveal its full form.

The paper is delicate. I test its strength gently, tugging on the edges, until a tiny tear begins to form. The sound is so jarring that I immediately release it and it flutters like a feather onto my lap.

I've heard the word paper before. It was once when I was little and my father was painting letters on a fiberglass board.

"A long, long time ago, they used letters to write down stories," he explained.

"Why don't we use them anymore?" Meghan asked.

"No one knows." My father shrugged. *"My grandmother, your great-great grandmother, used to say that we don't have the material for those stories anymore."*

"But you have paint," I pointed out. *"What other material do you need?"*

"Paint isn't everything, Brookie." He smiled. *"Stories needs lots and lots of words. They used to be written in*

things called books which were made up of many pages of paper."

"What's paper?" I'd asked.

"I don't really know what that is." My father shook his head. *"But I do know letters and you will too."*

"I don't see why we have to learn them," Meghan grumbled. *"No one else knows letters."*

"And all our stories are in our heads already," I sat by my sister's side on the floor and echoed her frustration. *"Well not the hard ones. The older people remember the hard ones for us, but we don't need those ancient books."*

"It's not about needing the books or being like everyone else." He crouched down so his face was directly in front of our faces. *"It's about gaining knowledge and learning that there are other ways of doing things."*

"That..." He stood up smiling and stretched out his back. *"And I'm your father so you don't get another choice."*

Meghan and I rolled our eyes, but we learned our letters and how to make them into words whether we liked it or not.

I pick up the paper tenderly, fully aware of how fragile it is. This object couldn't stand the test of time like the other materials in our world. Yet here it is in my hands. Another piece to the puzzle I need to solve.

It bothers me that Calder didn't copy the words to the parts that my father labeled, but I think I can remember most of them. It's the likeness of the painting that simultaneously fascinates and infuriates me. Calder was able to replicate the drawing of my father's machine in exact detail.

I roll onto my side and study the page. The light from the lantern shines through it. I jump off the bed and hold it against my mural. Through the paper I can make out the outline of the ship beneath it. Calder can't paint. He can only copy.

Satisfied that I have nothing in common with a watchman, I refold the paper and hide it behind my painting.

Despite my exhaustion, I toss and turn most of the night while diving between the dream world and reality. In my sleep, I see my father and Jillian. When I wake, I lay there trying to understand the connection. Both of them worked on devices that are unheard of in this world. Yet both of the devices were good and designed to help people.

Why would the watchmen take them for that? They weren't causing any trouble. Then again, if Meghan is right, maybe my father spoke out against the watchmen as Jillian had.

I bury my face into the pillow to try to stop my brain from spinning. Sleep doesn't come and my thoughts slip out as they test more theories.

It had something to do with the plans. My father had plans and Jillian's brother said a man came asking for advice on how to build the aquaponics system. But Jillian couldn't write or draw. *How could she have plans?* I turn to my back as the pieces of the puzzle slip in and out of place.

What else did they have in common? A man. Someone just passing through. Thomas told me at the repair shop that the only person who might be able to work on the machine was a traveler my father spoke of. I struggle to remember ever seeing or hearing about a traveler. Something tells me that I need to find out more about this man.

A snakelike figure dressed in black eludes my chase. I reach for it and tendrils of smoke lace through my fingers each time I draw back my hand.

"Look at me!" I scream but my voice only comes out as a subdued whisper. The figure laughs and turns around. Calder's piercing eyes haunt the remaining seconds of my dream.

*

"Hey." Lena steps inside the tavern kitchen just as I finish stacking the last of the clean plates on the shelf. Zoe leans against the sink picking at her nails. Her dress is soaked from washing the morning dishes, but I don't say anything because it's the first time I've ever seen her do them and I don't want it to be the last.

"I figured we could walk together to the spinners today." Lena wraps her arms over her chest as she lingers in the doorway.

"Sure." I nod to Zoe. "I think we are done with everything now." Zoe gives a short wave and leaves the kitchen without speaking. I've already grown used to her silent ways and kind of like her for them.

"You're getting close with her," Lena states as we step outside. The clean salt air fills my lungs and whips around my shoulders in a gentle breeze. It occurs to me that I haven't been out of the tavern since yesterday morning.

"We're not that close," I explain. "But we do live together."

"Hmm," Lena mumbles as she watches the merchants on the wharf call out their prices.

"What's wrong with you today?" I ask. "Are you still mad about our conversation the other night?"

"I spent last night with Tordon," she says softly.

"That would explain why you aren't worried that you haven't seen me in two days. But wait." I stop walking. "You spent the whole night with him?" Her cheeks flush. I've never seen that color on her before.

"Yes, the whole night," she whispers. I don't know whether to feel elated or confused. Both responses seem appropriate right now.

"Was it bad or something?" I ask.

"No." Her cheeks turn a deeper shade of red. "I just know you spent the night before last with him and I wasn't sure if…"

"Oh gods, no," I cut her off and pretend to gag. "I just couldn't leave them alone with Endre's body. I stayed to be with all of them."

"Oh okay," Lena sighs in relief. "I just wanted to make sure."

"Didn't Tordon tell you what happened?" I eye her warily.

"He did." She nods. "But I wanted to make sure that it was okay with you."

"Why wouldn't it be?" I exclaim as I lace my arm through hers. "So, are you two together now?"

"I don't know," Lena groans as she rubs her hand across her face. "He was so vulnerable last night and I wanted to do something to make him happy."

A fierce protectiveness takes me by surprise. "Promise me that you'll be honest about your feelings with him. I don't want him to get hurt."

Lena sighs. "I don't know what I'm getting myself into."

*

The songs of the spinners soften as Lena and I approach. The tune becomes a motherly hum, gentle and soothing like the one Aegir sang for Endre. I lower my face in embarrassment. They've changed the song for me.

"How are you doing, dear?" Margaret smiles as I take my place on the rocks beside Lena.

"I'm alright." My lips press together in a forced smile. "It's Aegir and the boys who need your kindness."

"Don't worry about that," Margert says. "We are taking shifts to help them."

"Thank you." I smile again, this time more sincerely as a small bit of weight lifts from my chest. The other women turn to nod at me respectfully and I shift uncomfortably on the rock. I know I'm supposed to be grateful for their empathy, but I've only done what any of us would do. I did the right thing. And that makes me sick to my stomach. How can anyone be okay in a world such as ours where not doing the right thing results in your disappearance?

"There's no watchmen here today." Lena nudges me as she directs my attention to the wharf.

"That's good," I mutter, even though it doesn't really matter anymore.

*

The tavern is mostly empty tonight. The street beneath my open window is quiet. I sit in the unfamiliar comfort of silence and allow myself to think.

There are too many open-ended questions swimming through my head. The weight of the unknown is so oppressing that it suffocates me. I need to paint.

The brush in my hand takes on a life of its own. Letters. I haven't painted letters in years. Not since I was a child. Not since my father forced me to learn. He'd be so proud of me now.

B's tail goes portside. D's tail goes starboard. There's a whole alphabet in there somewhere, but I don't need it all.

I dip the brush into the squid ink and pause. Images of my mother's hate filled eyes after she'd destroyed my mural flash through my mind.

Never mind that now. She's sailing away on a ship somewhere to live the rest of her retirement on the land. I wipe a tear from my cheek with my wrist and tell myself to be happy for her. It's easier to do that now that I know she didn't kill dad. I just wish I'd known sooner so I could have at least said goodbye.

Paint. Curves and lines and dots. Each letter painstakingly perfect, just the way that I was taught.

There are no absolute truths in this world, the letters say. I cake dark red paint from the crushed coral over them. The words lie. I remove the likeness of my father's sketch from behind the mural and hold it under my pillow as I fall asleep.

*

"Did you find what you were looking for?" Thomas asks as I step into his repair shop. The bell hasn't finished chiming as I lock the door behind me.

"No," I answer breathlessly. "I only found more questions."

"I can't help you then." He closes his tired eyes behind the broken spectacles.

"You have to," I argue. "I need to know what happened."

"I already told you more than enough. The machine was sabotaged. It wasn't my part that failed."

"But who would do such a thing and why?" I stand firmly in front of the counter. "I need to know more than this."

"I don't have those answers." He turns away from me and picks up a spool of tangled wire which he begins to straighten and rewrap.

"At least tell me about the drifter he hired," I beg. "What did he look like? How long did they work together?"

"I never met him," Thomas sighs. "Your father only spoke of him in passing once."

"Did he say anything important?" I ask. "Where he was from? What he was doing here? Anything that might help me find him."

Thomas removes his glasses and rubs his temple. "You aren't going to leave this alone, are you?"

"Never." I shake my head.

"I told you before, drifters never stick around. The man you are looking for is no longer here." He adjusts the glasses on his face again. "I can't think of anything important he said. The drifter was interested in his work and thought it could be used in other places. Once the machine was up and running, he was going to take the plans to another city to teach them how to make it."

"What did you say?" My heart stops beating for a moment and then wildly jumps inside my chest.

"I said that drifters never stay," Thomas starts.

"No." I place my hands atop the rusted metal counter. "What did you say about the plans?"

Thomas arches his silver-gray eyebrow. "You have them, don't you?"

The bluntness of the question catches me off guard. "Why would that matter?"

"It doesn't matter." Thomas swallows hard and studies my face looking for a truth I'm not ready to give him.

"Get rid of them," he demands.

"Why should I get rid of them?" I feign ignorance even as the guilt of the lie turns my stomach.

"Because it isn't safe to have them," he replies hastily. "And you need to leave now. I don't want this kind of trouble here."

I stare at the old man in wonder. He grows smaller under my gaze. There are secrets he is hiding, but I can press him no more. He's scared. As much as I want to force this, I won't be the cause for an old man's worries.

"Does your sister know what you're up to?" he calls as I unlock the door.

Meghan. I smile to myself. He's right. I need Meghan to tell me the whole truth.

*

"Auntie Brookie," Zander's familiar greeting rings in my ears as he leaps into my arms.

"Not now," I say gently after kissing him on his cheek. "I need to talk to your mama. She has something important she needs to tell me."

I've never been so abrupt with him. His arms hang limply at his sides as he walks to the back room. If things weren't the way they are, I'd beg for his forgiveness.

"What's gotten into you?" Meghan asks.

"Do you remember the drifter that dad had help him with his machine?" I turn to stare at my sister.

"Brooke." Her tone is warning. "I told you to let this go."

"Not a chance." I stand my ground. "I'm going to figure out what's happening."

"Nothing is happening." She enunciates each word carefully. "You are being paranoid. Please don't turn into our mother."

"You're lying to me." I refuse to sit in the chair she offers. "There is something you know that you aren't telling me."

"About some drifter?" She shakes her head and turns toward the kitchen. "I never met any drifter working with dad. I'm not lying."

"Not that." I follow her over to the stove, staring at her back and willing her to face me. "Why can't we question the watchmen?" The muscles of her shoulders tense.

"Because it's foolish," she whispers. "They are only here to protect the wall and keep us safe. When people start to question their intentions or methods it creates confusion and hatred. That's why the wall was built in the first place. You understand this as much as I do."

"What if I don't?" I fold my arms across my chest. "What if I think they are lying to us and we are all too stupid to see it? They killed our father. I know it."

"It's not stupidity." Meghan turns to me with pleading eyes. "And they didn't kill dad. Stop blaming them for that. This is the way things are and questioning it brings chaos. Please stop this, I'm begging you."

My sister isn't weak. She's the raging winds of a sea blown tempest, and that's just on her good days. To hear her speak like this confuses me. "What are you so scared of?"

Her eyes dart to the open door of the back room. "I'm scared of losing anyone I love," she says resolutely.

The revelation weighs heavily on me. I soften my voice. "I'm not trying to worry you. All I want is some answers and then I'll let it go."

"I don't have any answers," she sighs. "I never saw a drifter. I don't know what else you want to know."

"What did dad say about the watchmen?" I stare into my sister's eyes demanding the truth from her.

"It doesn't matter." She returns my stare.

"It does to me," I say. "Now tell me."

"Fine." Her nostrils flare. "You want to know what dad said? He said the same things you are saying. That something is wrong with the watchmen. That they shouldn't have the power to treat people this way and that we can take care of the wall ourselves."

"I knew it," I cry. "If you won't believe me, why can't you at least believe him?"

"Because dad is dead," she says flatly. "And I don't want you to be too. I've spent my whole life protecting you. What good did I do if I fail now?"

The silence that hangs in the air between us is punctuated by Thora fussing. Zander's small voice drifts out to the kitchen as he tries to comfort his little sister. Meghan and I share a smile.

"Have you taught him to read?" I ask absentmindedly as Thora begins to coo.

"I'm not sure that I will." Meghan bites her lip.

"Why wouldn't you?" My jaw drops. "Dad would have wanted you to teach him."

"What use is there for it?" She shrugs. "Don't you remember getting teased because we knew letters as kids? They said we were speaking gibberish. I don't want that for Zander."

"It wasn't that bad. They just thought we were a little weird." Thora's soft gurgles turn into screams and Meghan rushes to get her.

Zander skips out from behind his mother and meets me at the front door.

"Are you leaving?" He looks to me with sad eyes.

"I have to get to work." My lips pout to mirror his as I lean down to whisper, "But I promise to bring you a present the next time I come." He smiles brightly and wraps his arms around my waist.

"Hey, one more question," I call out to Meghan.

"What?" Her eyes dart to Zander's face.

I place my hands over his ears. "Did you notice anything different or out of place on the rocky outcropping the day that dad died?"

"What makes you think I was there?" Her forehead scrunches in confusion.

"Well, you picked up dad's bag and brought it home, didn't you?" I ask.

"No." She cocks her head to the side. It's the look she gives when she's trying to figure something out. "What makes you think that? It was already in the closet with his other things."

"Why would he leave it?" My question drifts unheard through the house as Thora demands her mother's full attention. I close the door behind me.

The wharf is busy today. I pass Anna and Bergah arguing over fish prices and quality much to the amusement of the customers, but I don't slow down to watch the debate.

Why would he leave his bag at home? It had all his tools in it. He never went anywhere without it. *Unless...* The sounds of the spinners grow louder as I approach the caves. *Unless he was worried that someone would find the plans.*

I force my racing pulse to slow as I sit on the rock and begin to work. Lena isn't here yet. She is always on time. Worry mixes with the heart wrenching dread that my father knew the plans were dangerous. He knew it, yet he made them anyway. *Did he know what was going to happen that day?*

The world around me begins to blur and I force myself to focus. Three twists and a knot. I need to work.

"What's bothering you child?" Margaret's knees crack as she sits on the rock beside me.

The whole world, I don't say.

"Come on now," she teases. "Something is on that pretty little mind of yours. I've never seen you this focused. Is it Aegir's son?"

Endre. How easily I'd forgotten about him. *Does that make me a bad person?* I nod.

"It's hard when we don't end up with the ones we love," Margaret sighs.

"What?" I ask, taken aback. "Oh, you mean Tordon. I'm not worried about him."

"No?" She glances at me. "Then what is it?"

I take a second to look at her, and I mean really look. She's older than my grandmother would be and yet she never chose to retire. Besides working with the spinners, she's also one of the city's midwives. She was there for my and Meghan's birth. She was there for Zander and would have been for Thora had the storm not raged that night.

Her fingers are stiff as she works the plastic strip between them, but I've never seen a hint of pain on her face. Plus, she helped my mother. On that attribute alone I should trust her.

"Do you ever feel like something is wrong?" I ask softly.

She looks me over with calculating eyes. "Are you not feeling well, child?"

"No," I hurry to reassure her. "Nothing like that. I mean with this world and the way we live." I lower my voice to add, "With the watchmen."

"By the gods." Margaret smiles. "You sure do think a lot. You're just like your father."

"Not really." I shake my head. "He was smart enough to know things. He had a plan to fix the world. All I have are questions with no answers."

"How do you think he got to that point?" Margaret chuckles. I stare at her silently, wanting to know more.

"He made many mistakes," she confides in me, "but he never stopped asking questions."

"Everyone says my questions are foolish." Angry tears well in my eyes. "They are telling me to stop asking them."

"That's what is wrong with the world if you want my opinion." Margaret stretches her back and lets out a groan. "Everyone is afraid to ask. Or maybe they are afraid of the answer. What does your heart tell you to do?"

"I want to know the truth." There is no other response I can give this question.

"Even if knowing is dangerous?" She stares me in the eye. There's a youthful vigor behind the creeping opaque of her iris, a spark that is so very much alive.

"Yes." I smile. "No matter the cost. I need to know."

"Keep asking questions then." She winks. "Either you'll find the answers or they will find you."

"Sorry I'm late!" Lena gushes, breaking the intensity of the conversation. "I was helping Aegir and lost track of time."

Margaret nods at Lena and gives me a final smile before hoisting herself off the rock and returning to her own place. I pretend not to notice the purple blotches that have formed on Lena's neck.

"Helping Aegir?" I ask playfully.

"Well," Lena giggles, "helping one of his sons."

"You like him, don't you?"

"Honestly? I think I always did." Lena shrugs. "But you two had your thing and I never would have intruded on that."

"It wasn't a thing," I groan in embarrassment. "We had one awkward moment where we took our friendship to the next level and it was so very wrong."

"I know that now, silly." Lena bumps against me. "I just wanted to make sure."

"You two will be good together," I say sincerely. "It was meant to be."

We busy ourselves in the spinning plastic, twirling and knotting until our calloused fingers go numb. Out of habit, I steal glances at the wharf throughout the evening, but no watchmen make their appearance.

At the end of our shift, once our work is stored away, Lena laces her arm through mine and we climb toward the wharf. Tordon is there waiting.

"Hey Brooke." He smiles politely, but his face is turned toward Lena. She tries to subdue her excitement, but a giggle escapes untethered from her lips and she claps her free hand over her mouth to hide it. The current between the two of them is nauseating.

"Hey Tordon." I return his simple smile. "How are you doing?" The trance breaks as he glances at me.

"Not awful, considering..." His voice trails off, but his eyes reignite when he looks back to Lena. *This is really uncomfortable.* I force myself to continue smiling.

"Would you mind walking Lena home?" I blurt out. They both turn to stare at me. "I left something at the caves. Plus, I'd kind of like some alone time." It's only half a lie.

Lena tightens her grip on my arm. "Are you sure about this?" she asks. Her eyes are pleading. I can read her face as clear as ever, she doesn't want anything to change between us.

"I'm sure." I nudge her forward. "It's just for tonight. I have a lot on my mind."

Tordon and Lena grasp hands, but he turns to me before they leave. "There was something I wanted to talk to you about, Brooke." He pauses as if unsure of where he is. "Since we have tomorrow off, I'm going to the wrecking yard to see what was salvaged of the boat. Did you still want to come along?"

"Of course." I rush to add, "All three of us should go. I mean, if you want to come too, Lena."

She nods. Her eyes never leave Tordon's face. The sight of her brings a warm feeling that fills the pit of my stomach even as my eyes threaten to roll. I don't think I've ever seen her this way. It's a good look on her.

"I'll probably have to work the morning shift at the tavern because I missed a few days," I explain. "But I'll meet you there, after."

"That's perfect." Tordon smiles as he looks down at Lena's adoring face. "I'd love to sleep in tomorrow."

I left nothing with the spinners. Still, I climb back down the rocks and check that Lena has left with Tordon before I make my way back up again.

☦ CHAPTER FOUR ☦

The lanterns are already lit. Darkness is coming earlier now. The cold will be here soon. Not miserable cold like the stories fishermen tell of the northern waters, but colder than we are used to for the rest of the year.

I'm glad I have my father's jacket. The rest of my winter clothes were left in my childhood home. There's no chance that I'll be able to go back there and claim anything. Good houses go quick, and I know my mother wouldn't have made any provisions to leave anything to Meghan or me.

I remind myself to ask Margaret if mother gave the house to anyone or if someone just snatched it up. I hope it's a family with children who will grow up laughing within those walls.

"Open up, you sea siren." The deep voice of a man echoes down the empty wharf. If the lanterns are lit, it should be quiet now. No one should be causing a commotion. A metal door vibrates against the pounding of a fist.

"You think you are better than me, don't you? Just because you make shady deals with the fishermen."

I turn the corner to see Bergah leaning against the back of Anna's shop as his large knuckles beat against the doorframe.

"Go away, you lousy drunk," Anna's strong voice calls sternly from inside. "I'm tired of you coming around here with your nonsense. Leave me alone. It's not my fault your fish are rotten."

Anna's words seem to enrage him. He slams his palm against the wall and then cradles it to his chest as he lets out a loud belch. "Oh Anna, don't tease me like this. You know I love you and you didn't say these things the other night."

A smile teases the corner of my lips. *They have such a weird relationship.*

Suddenly, a group of watchmen seem to materialize out of thin air. Three more push past me to join the group forming around Bergah.

"Hey, wait a minute," Bergah stutters as the first watchman places his hand on his arm. "I wasn't causing any trouble."

"That's not what it looks like," a cold voice speaks from the faceless crowd of men. Their uniformed bodies fill the dimly lit walkway. The more of them that arrive, the harder it is to see Bergah's face. Confusion freezes me where I stand. *Was he really doing anything wrong?*

"No!" Bergah screams as the watchmen begin to move him. He lashes out at the circle with his fists causing it to momentarily break and then form tighter once more.

"I'm begging you, please don't do this!" he cries as the cluster pushes forward.

"Wait." My voice springs from my throat with no logic to the action. "You can't take him. He didn't do anything wrong."

"Listen to her," Bergah pleads. "I was only teasing Anna. We always tease each other."

"This isn't the first time you've caused a scene," another watchman speaks, "and it seems like she's had enough."

"Can we get Anna to decide?" I try to force my way through the crowd of watchmen to get to the center and find whoever is leading this operation. Rough hands grab the tops of my shoulders and pull me back out of the crowd into the shadows of the walkway.

"Be quiet," Calder commands as he pushes me off the main path.

"No." I try to pry his fingers from my skin. "You need to let Anna decide if he is causing trouble. They always act like this to one another." I raise my voice hoping the other watchmen will take notice. Calder places his hand firmly over my mouth.

"You don't have a lick of sense, do you?" he whispers harshly into my ear. I struggle to break free from his grasp and trip over the raised plank of a shop's doorstep. Calder doesn't let me fall. He just moves me over the stupid plank like I'm weightless and half carries me into the shadows.

"Let go of me!" I demand.

"Gladly." He shoves me away and I spin around to face him. We've turned so far down the side walkways that I can no longer see the main wharf. I rush forward intending to return to Bergah's defense, but he steps in front of me blocking the path.

"What is wrong with you?" I scream in frustration.

"Me?" He raises his eyebrows. "What is wrong with you? I told you to stay out of trouble and here you are wildly screaming in the dark sticking your nose where it doesn't belong. I thought maybe you were smarter than this, but I guess I was wrong."

"You don't know anything about me," I spit. "Now get out of my way."

"No." He crosses his arms over his chest. "You need to go home now."

"What I need to do is stop your people from taking an innocent life." I glare at him.

"My people?" He returns my stare intently.

"Yes." The word forces its way through the cracks of my clenched teeth. "You overbearing, ignorant watchmen."

"Ignorant," he chuckles coldly. "Do you even know what that word means?"

"Do you know what the word asshole means?" My vision blurs from hatred.

"Hey now." He shrugs as his lips raise in a sarcastic smile. "I'm just doing my job."

"I don't care what you are doing." I stand on my tiptoes so that we are at eye level. "Get out of my way."

"Fine." He steps aside. I don't wait for him to second guess it. I bolt past him and run down the walkways as fast as my legs will carry me. The wharf is empty when I get there.

"Anna!" I beat against the door frantically. The pounding of my fists makes much less noise than Bergah's did moments earlier. "Please, Anna, open up. They are taking Bergah away. We have to do something to stop them."

"She's not going to open the door," Calder sighs, suddenly right beside me. I ignore him and press my ear to the cool metal siding. From inside the shack comes the faintest whimper of a woman crying.

"Please Anna." I knock again. "We have to do something to help." She doesn't respond.

"Let this go," Calder says solemnly. "Let's just get you home."

Tears stream down my face and my breath hitches in painful gasps. "Where are they taking him?"

"To our ship of course," Calder states. He isn't even bothering to lie to me.

"What will they do to him on your ship?" The emotions slowly drain from me like the tide ebbing back out to sea.

"He'll be tried and found guilty of disturbance." Calder shrugs. "Then his body will be released into the ocean in the traditional burial manner."

I swallow hard. There is no doubt in mine or anyone's mind that this is what happens if you disappear, but to hear it spoken aloud and so calmly causes chills to run up my spine.

"What if we can get a witness in his defense?" I ask hopefully and turn to knock again. "Anna, please come out. We still have a chance to save him."

"You have no chance." Calder places his big hand over my fist and holds it still. "This was his final chance."

Tears drip down my cheeks. "I don't understand."

"Of course you don't." Calder shakes his head sadly and studies my face. I don't blink. He hesitates as if finding the right words to say. "He's been watched for a long time. These episodes are sporadic and unpredictable. According to the previous rotation of watchmen, it's been eight months since the last incident. He gets drunk and causes a ruckus, usually beating at this poor old woman's door. It was time to put an end to it. Who knows when he'll take it too far?"

"You don't understand." I point my finger at his chest. "This is just how he is. It's how most of us are. It's just teasing. He would never hurt her. They've been acting this way since I was a child."

"And we've decided it needs to stop," he says calmly.

"Who are you to make that decision?" I raise my fist to knock again. "Anna should be the one deciding if she's had enough."

"She's already made her decision." Calder motions to the door. "The woman is too scared to come out and engage with you."

"She's not scared of me," I protest in outrage. "She's scared of you and of all the watchmen. She's afraid of what will happen if she speaks out."

"That might be true," Calder says. "But we are only doing what is right. I wouldn't expect someone like you to be able to understand."

"Someone like me?" I bite my lip so hard it hurts. We stare at each other in silence. There are so many things I want to scream at this man, but it won't do anything to help. He already thinks he is better than me.

"Anna." I knock softly. "We can save him if you help me."

"Go away," Anna's pain-stricken voice calls from the other side of the door.

"You heard her," Calder whispers. "It's time for you to go home."

I pause, unsure of what to do, but Calder is right. Without Anna I can't fight this. Causing a scene here will just put me in the same position as Bergah. I can't do that, not until I know the truth.

*

"I know where I'm going." I turn my head to glare over my shoulder as Calder follows me to the tavern.

"Are you sure about that?" he asks coldly. "You seem to get sidetracked easily."

My tongue sits inside my cheek as I force myself to take one step after the other away from Anna and away from helping Bergah. Gertrude is sure to yell at me if she sees a watchman escorting me home.

"Stop." I spin around to face him as the tavern comes into view. "I don't want the drama of you stalking me. I swear I'm going to my room."

"Good." Calder nods and turns to leave. "I don't want to be here anyway."

"Wait," I call out. The lantern lit walkways are empty. The only sign of life on the wharf comes from the noises within the tavern. Calder slips into the shadows and there he stands. The truest form of himself. "Where are you from? Where do they still make paper?"

"Nowhere," his voice is distant. "It's an old relic."

"Stop that." I walk deeper into the shadows until I'm face to face with him. "I want to know the truth."

"Down south," he answers mechanically.

"You're a liar." I glare at him.

"Believe what you want." He turns away.

"Wait," I say again. "I have so many questions. If you could just stop being rude and answer them, I'll keep my head down. I swear."

"I gave you an answer. Now stop asking questions," he smirks.

"Never." I smile challengingly, remembering Margaret's stories of my father. "Why didn't you copy the names of the parts on the painting you gave me?"

The muscles in his jaw tense under the weak lantern glow. "I didn't think it was important. I assumed you couldn't read them."

"Of course I know how to read." I study his face. "Do you?"

"Go to sleep." His words drift to me through the stillness of the night as he walks away. "And stop being stupid unless you want to disappear."

I hate him. The tavern is full of people celebrating the last workday of the week. Yet the joyous sounds do nothing to temper the boiling of blood inside my ears. *He is a liar. They are all liars.*

Gertrude is too busy filling drinks at the bar to notice me stomp past her and up the stairs. Once the door is locked behind me, I clench my teeth to stop from screaming. If I don't paint right now, I'll go running down the walkway to where the off-duty watchmen linger in the loft and demand the truth from them. *I need to paint.*

"Our little secret." My father chops off a lock of my hair and fastens it to the metal pole.

"Will mama be mad that we cut my hair?" I ask in a childish whisper.

"Shh." He smiles. *"Don't you worry about what your mama thinks. Let me handle her."*

"Who do we need to keep secrets from?" I stare at the new paintbrush in wonder.

"From everyone you can't trust." He winks playfully. *"No one here understands what painting is. They don't need to know your secrets."*

Brown. My hair is brown. Like brown seaweed drying in the sun. It's the same color hair that my father and sister have. My lips are faded conch shell pink. The color of my mother's lips. My shoulders and my legs are strong. I have my mother's hands and my father's feet. I stare at my eyes in the cracked mirror on the wall. They don't look like the ones I've always known.

Down the curve of my back, the paintbrush slips. Just a little imperfection.

There I am. It's me, including the flaws, standing in the storm of my painting. My first self-portrait. I chuckle sarcastically as I drop the brushes into the wash basin. I don't know who this girl is anymore, but I make a silent promise that I'll find out.

*

"Do you need anything else?" I nervously wring my hands as I stand in front of Gertrude in the kitchen. The morning shift is over, but I don't want to anger my landlord and employer by rushing off after the events of the past few days. "I'm meeting up with Tordon to visit the remains of the *Hronn*."

Her eyes are full of pity. I flinch at the look she gives. If there is one thing I know about myself, it's that I can't stand sympathy. At least that hasn't changed.

"Go on, child," she says softly. "Let me know if you need anything."

I swallow down my pride and force a smile. "I'll pass along your sentiments to Aegir and Tordon."

The wharf is full of laughter. Everyone has the day off to shop and lounge around. I used to love the weekends. Now the amount of people crowding the walkways is annoying. I'd like to move faster than they allow.

There's an opening near Bergah's closed shop. Everyone gives it a wide berth today. I remember he had brothers. Maybe one of them will open the stall tomorrow. I slip away from the crowd and try to get ahead.

Anna is nowhere to be seen. The girl that helps on weekends frantically tries to manage the customers and handle orders. A young boy pockets a handful of clams from the bucket at the front. I smack the back of his head and his face goes red. He regretfully empties his pockets returning the shellfish to its rightful place. The girl gives me an appreciative smile as I hurry away.

"There you are." Lena pulls her hand from Tordon's elbow and wraps her arms around me. "We were about to go looking for you."

"Am I late?" I hug her tightly and glance at Tordon over her shoulder.

His eyes shift to the planks beneath us. "Not really. We just got here."

"Oh good." I give him a big smile. "But, how are you? Are you sure you are okay with seeing this?"

"Yeah." His answer is flat. "I need to see what happened."

The cranes are still attached to the *Hronn* as she sits on the floating docks of the wrecking yard. Soon she'll be stripped, torn apart bit by bit, and even her bones will be repurposed elsewhere. They haven't picked her apart just yet. I'm tempted to ask Tordon if he told them to wait, but the pain in his eyes silences me.

Staring at this twisted boat is horrifying. The *Hronn's* hull is smashed in where it crashed against the rocks. The stern sits lower than should be possible as it holds the weight of the destruction.

Tordon goes first, reaching for the steps and hoisting himself up onto what remains of the deck.

"Should we give him a minute?" Lena whispers in my ear. Any other day I'd say yes, but I need to see this too.

"Maybe it's better if we don't leave him alone right now." I grab the metal rung that hangs next to the remaining steps.

Tordon stands on the broken mess of a boat silently taking it all in. I don't have the heart to offer more than half a hug right now. Lena comes up behind me and laces her fingers through his. I feel guilty that I'm not the one he finds comfort in after all our years together. He sighs as he leans against Lena. *This is good,* I tell myself. *He needs all the support he can get.*

Slowly, I edge away from them while walking the unnatural incline of the deck. Nothing seems out of place, but I'm not sure what I'm looking for.

I climb down to the cabin. There's no blood, no sign of struggle except the twisted metal and hanging wires where the boat caved in. The cabinet doors are still locked. No one ransacked them. My eyes dart around the wreckage looking for the rest of the rope. *If it was tied around his neck accidently, or on purpose, shouldn't the evidence be here somewhere?*

"They're not here," Tordon whispers behind my back causing my heart to leap out of my chest.

"What's not here?" I ask as my breathing returns to its normal rate.

"The gas cans." He turns to climb up the ladder.

"Wait." I reach for his arm and pull him back. "Why do you care about the gas cans?"

"It's just a weird suspicion I had. Don't worry about it." He clenches his fist as he stares at the damage on the ceiling.

"Yeah right." I roll my eyes. "Since when do you not tell me the truth?"

"Since you stopped talking to me for a few months." His words hurt. He wants them to hurt because he is hurting.

"I never really apologized for that," I say softly. "I wish I had the voice then to say what I felt."

"I don't really blame you," he sighs. "You were never one to speak in your own defense. It's like you accepted the hand you were dealt and never questioned anything."

"Well, I have questions now." I shrug. "What's so important about the gas cans?" Tordon looks at the wrecked cabin and then back to the stairs. I almost expect him to leave without answering me.

"My father is missing gas cans," he suddenly whispers. "I'm almost positive they were on the boat with Endre the night he went out fishing."

"Okay." I stare at him waiting for the meaning behind his words to emerge. Aegir is rich. He can afford fuel to supplement the sails of his ships. Having gas cans on the boat isn't weird. "Why aren't the gas cans here?"

"Maybe they fell into the water." Tordon closes his eyes. I stand silently as he talks this out. "That doesn't make sense. They'd be secured below deck. I think he may have gone to fill them and something must have happened."

"What could have happened?" I struggle to understand where this is going. "What's at the fuel station that would cause you to worry like this?"

"Nothing." He shakes his head as he surveys the damage of the cabin once more. "It's just a fuel station. The watchmen exchange gas for whatever goods my father provides."

I try to quell the rising panic in my chest. "The watchmen run the fuel station too?"

"They run everything," he answers bitterly. Panic turns to anger as I swallow this information.

"Did you have a chance to talk to Aegir before this happened?" I ask. "Did you tell him about my plan to get rid of the watchmen?"

"I did." He turns to face me and his eyes stare straight into mine. We've been friends since before I can remember. Lena and I are close like sisters, but

I've always had a different kind of bond with Tordon. He knows what I am thinking when I can't articulate my response. We'd always thought alike. The look we share now is nothing from our innocent youth. There's no playful mischief, no inside joke. His eyes mirror the rage in my own.

"Aegir won't help us," he says coldly. "The risks are too high and he has responsibilities he can't break."

"But we don't." I look to him for reassurance.

"No, we don't." He smiles.

"Should I come down?" Lena calls from above deck. Her musical voice breaks the ice from the conversation.

"Don't worry about it," Tordon calls. "We are coming up now." The change in his tone is jarring until I remember their newly found connection. Tordon doesn't wait for me as he turns to climb the steps. I give them a moment alone as I take one last look around the cabin. Whatever tragedy befell Endre didn't happen on this boat.

*

"I'd like to visit the fuel station sometime," I slip this request casually into the conversation as we climb down from the *Hrønn* into the wreckage yard.

"I think I want to go visit it myself," Tordon says absentmindedly.

"What's at the refueling station?" Lena asks. Tordon blanches and I walk backwards smiling at the two of them.

"You might as well tell her everything," I laugh. "If you don't, then I will."

✝ CHAPTER FIVE ✝

There's one more place I need to go today even though I really don't ever want to go back there. Jillian's shop, or I guess its Shane's shop now, is still boarded up. I stand knocking at the door for a few minutes until the lock finally unlatches.

"What do you want?" Shane's wide eyes quickly scan the walkway behind me. The stench of the house smacks me in the face as it drifts out into the clean salty sea air. I inhale through my mouth and try my hardest not to shudder.

"Do you mind if we talk for a second?" I ask.

"I don't have anything to say." He moves to close the door.

"Please." I say the word as sweetly as I can manage while only breathing through my lips. "I just want to ask you a simple question and then I'll never bother you again."

"Fine." He grits his teeth. The door opens wide and I gasp involuntarily as the full stench of the rotten produce escapes. He closes the door behind him as he steps outside. I've never been more relieved in my life.

"What is it?" he whispers anxiously.

I decide to be blunt. "The man who came to talk to Jillian about the growing system, have you ever seen him before? Is he still around?"

Shane lowers his head. "It doesn't matter."

"It matters to me." I gently move his chin up so he looks at me again. "A drifter spoke to my father too. Now my father is dead. There's a connection between the two of them that I need to understand."

Shane flinches. "I want no part of this."

"I'm not asking for you to play a part." I smile reassuringly. "I'm just asking about the drifter."

His eyes shift as he thinks. Whatever he is working up the courage to tell me will be a lie. That's one of the perks of staying silent and watching for most of my life. I know how people act. Coming here was a mistake. Jillian would have told me the truth, but sometimes siblings are nothing alike.

"I don't know anything about him," he says. "Drifters come and go all the time." I was expecting this answer so I don't get angry.

"Can you at least tell me what he looked like?" I plead. "Maybe then I can keep an eye out for him."

"He was just a man." Shane shrugs. "I didn't see him clearly."

"I don't understand why you won't help me." Tears of frustration well in my eyes. I don't know why everyone is this scared all the time. *What does he have left to lose?* Shane's face contorts as he studies my reaction. I don't want his sympathy.

"Hang on," he says as I turn to leave. "He was tall and had a crooked nose."

Rage forms a hard pit in my stomach. The wind from the ocean dries the tears on my face. "Was his name Henry?" I ask calmly.

"I didn't catch his name," Shane begins to stutter. "That's all I know. I shouldn't even be talking to you." The door slams and locks behind me.

*

The tavern is the tallest building in the city. It's two stories high. No one builds structures taller than this because they aren't able to withstand the storms. The tavern is as wide as it is tall, a perfect square. There were once tall buildings called sky scrapers that are buried deep within the sea.

Divers used to love them because they were easily accessed when scavenging, but the ones that have been marked are picked clean now. The empty shells of buildings are nothing more than a nuisance to boats that try to navigate the waters.

I keep my eyes fixated on the window of my room in the tavern as I walk dreamlike through the crowds of people enjoying their day off. I already miss the rocky outcropping where my father's machine once sat. Maybe in a few days I'll force myself to go back there. I liked that it was my place to be alone. Sure, it wouldn't exist if the machine had worked and my father was still alive to see his dream of making land come true. But I found comfort in being able to go somewhere to get away from everything.

There is no running from this now. I need to talk to Aegir. He has to know that Henry can't be trusted. The way he addressed him the night they brought Endre's body home was too familiar. Henry didn't tell him about the rope. I don't know why I thought he seemed gentle. The man is a liar living a double life. Why would a watchman want to pretend to be a drifter?

Unless he was a spy. I hesitate at the tavern door and cast a worried glance over my shoulder. Are there other spies out there? Is this why people are scared to talk? My eyes open wide in surprise. *No.* I force the paranoid thoughts away. We know each other. We'd know if someone wasn't one of us.

Then again, Aegir seemed to know Henry. *Does Aegir know what happened to my father?* I refuse to believe that. Aegir and my father were friends. My hands shake as I push open the door.

"There you are," Lena laughs when I walk into the kitchen. Rupert is loading up her plate with blackened fish from the stove and he motions for me to grab another dish.

"Becca is sick," Gertrude grumbles as the swinging door to the kitchen opens. "Where is…" She looks up to see me standing there and claps her hands together. "Brooke. Perfect. I'll need your help tonight. You girls hurry and eat. Shorter days mean more customers. I'm going to have to hire extra help." The door swings closed again and Gertrude continues her one-sided conversation on the other side.

"I guess you're working with me tonight," Lena giggles as Rupert hands me dinner.

"I guess so," I sigh.

Shorter days mean there is less to do. The tavern makes enough to keep the lights on and burning bright throughout the darkness of the evening. Around the holidays, Gertrude hires weekly entertainment from the extra profit shorter days bring in. I'm grateful I never had to spend winter nights alone locked in my childhood home with my mother. I'd have probably ended up as crazy as she is.

For a moment I let myself imagine that she's comfortably sitting on the land somewhere, maybe under an apple tree or something. I hope that is true for her. Maybe she is finally happy.

The night wears on as the crowd of diners linger longer than normal to enjoy the warmth of the tavern. They eat their food slower and their conversations continue long after we remove their dirty dishes.

The first wave of off duty watchmen enter just as I finish wiping down my empty tables. Lena groans apologetically as she struggles under the weight of her tray.

"Don't worry, I'll take care of them." I give her a reassuring smile before turning to climb the stairs.

"What will it be tonight, gentlemen?" I raise my voice to be heard above the watchmen's chatter. It seems they've already forgotten I exist. Well, everyone except Calder. His shoulders are tight as he focuses on the table in front of him. I ask the question again louder.

"Food, please," Drake orders for the group. "Whatever the cook is frying up smells a hundred times better than the food on ship tonight." The other watchmen chuckle at his joke. Even Calder smiles. I quickly take a headcount.

"Beers too, I'm assuming?" I ask.

"Of course, darling." Drake gives me a charming smile. "And maybe your friend can help bring them up."

*

"Are you okay?" Lena bustles into the kitchen as I'm giving the order to Rupert.

"Yes." I shrug. "Why wouldn't I be?"

Lena arches an eyebrow as she studies my expression. "Because it's the watchmen and they bother you."

There's so much I haven't told her lately. I feel like an awful friend. We haven't had a minute alone together in what feels like forever.

"They don't bother me anymore." I shake my head. *Hate is so much stronger than fear.*

"That's good." Lena takes my hand and gives it a gentle squeeze. "I told you there was nothing to worry about." My jaw drops, but now isn't the time to tell her everything.

"I'll take care of them tonight," I say. "Drake keeps asking for you."

"Oh yeah," Lena groans. "Maybe I should tell him about Tordon. This whole relationship thing is weird. What are the rules?" she asks me like I know.

"Flirting with other men isn't the best way to be faithful to one guy," Rupert interjects into our conversation. "It's a good way to cause problems and break trust."

We both turn to him in confusion. At times, it's easy to forget he is even here. He hardly ever speaks. How much has he heard about us when we didn't realize he was listening?

"Rupert might be right," I laugh.

"Maybe." Lena nods. "Let me talk to Tordon and see what he thinks."

I leave her chewing her lip, lost in thought, as I carry the first tray up the steps.

"Your food, sir," I smirk as I set a plate in front of Calder.

"Thank you," he responds bitterly.

"Where's our beautiful friend?" Drake drapes his arm across my shoulders and looks over the balcony to the tavern floor. "I was hoping she'd come pay me a visit." I shrug him off and pick up the tray.

"She's working," I explain. "It's a busy night tonight. Is there anything else you need?"

"Can you tell her I'll buy her a drink later in the evening when the crowd dies down?" Drake asks.

"That's probably not going to happen." I shake my head sympathetically. I never knew I was this good of an actress. "Her boyfriend is picking her up."

"Boyfriend you say." Drake rubs his knuckles slowly over his lips and then grins. "Well, that's alright. Why don't you let me buy you a drink later?"

"No thank you." I smile brightly. "I've got better things to do."

Calder spits out some of his beer as he chuckles and then quickly covers the outburst with a cough. I don't turn back to glare at him like I want to.

*

"Oh, I didn't realize he was actually coming to get you," I laugh when Tordon walks into the kitchen.

"What?" Lena asks looking up from the soapy water. Her eyes light up when she sees him standing there. My heart is happy for the two of them. Tordon puts his hands in his pockets and smiles at her.

"I actually came to ask if you'd both like to take a boat ride with me in the morning," he explains. "Then I was hoping I could walk you home."

Lena nods. "Yes to both."

I was hoping she would stay a while to talk with me tonight, but how can I say anything when they both look this annoyingly cute?

"Yes to the boat ride." I nudge Lena with my hip, shoving her away from the sink. "I'll finish up here so that you can walk her home. Now go away before you two make me throw up."

*

Tordon sets the sails. The wind is perfect today. All our boats are fitted with sails. Even if you maintain the engine, and even if you can afford fuel like Aegir can, you still use gas sparingly.

The sun glitters off the ripples in front of us and the white caps of our wake distort the perfect calm of the water. I walk to the bow to watch the horizon.

There's nothing out here. It's just miles and miles of endless water that drops off at the edge of the world. The world could be flat if this was all you knew, but we know better. Our ancestors taught us that the earth is round and if you are brave enough to spend years at sea, we could even travel around it. The old ones say that you could see how round the earth was when they shot large ships into the sky. It still amazes me that there was once so much knowledge, so much technology, and all of it lays drowned beneath us.

The rock of the boat is calming. I stand alone on the deck leaning over the guardrails. A single gannet dives beneath the surface. I anxiously wait for his return and am not disappointed. Moments later, he reemerges from the depths of the sea with water dripping from his black tipped feathers and a mackerel held securely in his beak.

The sea is dangerous, but she is so beautiful. If the wind wasn't propelling us forward at this speed then I'd lower down and let my fingers trail along the current so the silkiness of the water could dance against my skin. As much as I love the colors of the earth, I'd be lying if I didn't admit that I'd be lost without the powerful calm of the ocean. Honestly, most of us would.

"Ugh." Lena leans over the rail beside me and vomits.

"How have you never been on a boat before?" Tordon chuckles as he holds her hair away from her face.

"Can you not say the word boat again?" She glares at him. I laugh and she clings to my arm while wiping spit from her chin. "Nothing about this is funny."

"It's a little funny." I smile. "We literally live on the ocean and you somehow get seasick."

"You're a brat." She stands up straight. "Just because I live here doesn't mean I want to sail out on it."

"Feel better?" I ask as I wrap my arm around her waist.

"A little." She narrows her eyes. "Am I supposed to stay mad the entire trip?"

I sway from side to side and instantly stop when her forehead starts to sweat. "Yep. Just stay mad."

"And how exactly am I supposed to do that?" Lena groans.

"I think I can help," I say solemnly. "There are some things you both need to know."

I spend the next thirty minutes catching Tordon and Lena up on everything that has happened for the past few days. Jillian's and Bergah's disappearance, the things that Calder has said. Tordon's knuckles turn white as he grips the rails when he learns of the rope around Endre's neck. I even tell them about the paper. There is no guilt in speaking the truth. It's freeing in an unimaginable way to be able to talk this honestly without the fear of anyone eavesdropping.

"What do you think all of this means?" Lena looks like she's going to be sick again, but it's no longer from the rocking of the waves.

"It means the watchmen are not who they say they are." Tordon breaks his silence and turns to face me. "But I think I've always known that."

"We need to talk to your father," I say. "He knows who Henry is. He must know more about the watchmen in general. Maybe he can help us get rid of them."

"Get rid of them." Lena's eyes are wide as she looks between the two of us. "Are you crazy? What are you even talking about?"

"It's not going to work." Tordon shakes his head. "I tried talking to him the morning they found Endre when we were fishing. He said there were things I'm better off not knowing and wouldn't discuss it further. He made me promise to leave it alone."

"What are we doing now?" I raise my palms in the air. "It doesn't seem like you are leaving anything alone."

"I don't know what I'm doing," Tordon sighs. "I just wanted to see it for myself. But I recognized Henry too that night. He and my father did some work together when I was a child. You would have seen him the day I did. We were playing on the docks when he showed up."

"Was he in a watchman's uniform?" I ask, straining my memory to recall what day he is speaking of and coming up short.

"No." Tordon runs a hand through his hair as he stares out at the sea. "He was dressed like one of us. I honestly wouldn't have made the connection if you didn't bring it up."

"Maybe he is from here," Lena tries to rationalize. "He could have been wearing regular clothes to visit his family."

"That would make sense," I say, "but it doesn't explain his connection to Jillian's disappearance."

"When you are looking for a connection you can find one anywhere. This talk of getting rid of the watchmen is insane. You are both freaking me out." Lena storms across the deck and Tordon rushes to follow her. I'm left alone with my thoughts. *Am I making connections that don't exist?* It's possible. I just know I need to ask these questions because if I don't, who will?

*

I don't know what I was expecting to find at the fuel station. There's a five-man crew standing guard with their ancient weapons at the loading dock. The sight of the machines in their hands pointed at us is as terrifying as it is meant to be.

"Good afternoon gentlemen," Tordon calls out a friendly greeting as we approach. "I was just in the area and figured I'd stop by for a little chat if you have the time."

"What is this about?" the watchmen closest to us barks.

"You know my brother, Endre, right?" Tordon lowers his head letting his shaggy hair hang over his eyes and slumps his shoulders forward. He's putting on some kind of show. "Well, he passed away a few days ago. Come to think of it, it was the day he was supposed to come here. I was just wondering if you got a chance to see him. You might have heard his last words."

"I don't know what you are talking about son," the watchman responds. "I'm sorry for your loss, but if you don't have the authorization to be here then you need to leave."

The other watchmen snap to attention and point their weapons at us. It's only the lanky boy in the too big uniform standing near the back that doesn't meet our eyes. I lean over the railing to get a better look at the young watchman.

"Hey you," I call out. "Yes, you at the edge of the dock. Did you see a boy about your age come through here the other day?" He raises his face just enough to show me the blush of his cheeks as he shakes his head.

"He's lying," I mouth to Tordon.

"It's time for you to go now," the watchman states.

"Alright." Tordon raises his hands in surrender. "We're leaving. If you happen upon his gas cans, would you mind returning them to me?"

The watchman stand silently as Tordon turns us around. Once we've drifted for a few miles, he angrily ties up the sails and switches on the motor. The roar of the engine is deafening.

"Will your father be mad at you for using fuel?" I call out.

"He lost a son for this precious fuel. Do you think I care if he is upset now?" Tordon grips the wheel tightly and we propel like a bird gliding over the waves.

Lena sits above deck where the engine isn't as loud. The spray of the water mists her face while she stares ahead at the shoreline.

"How are you feeling?" I ask as I sit beside her. "Are you still sick?"

"No." Lena doesn't look at me. "It's better now that I can see where I am going."

"Where are you going?" I ask playfully. She's never been one to speak in riddles.

"I'm going home. My mother and my sisters need me." It's an honest answer. I wouldn't expect anything less.

"It doesn't bother you that we are being lied to?" I make the question soft.

"Yes, it does." There are tears in her eyes when she turns to me. "But I won't jeopardize the ones I love to stay on this crazy path."

"I really do understand you," I say. "It's just that I can't live like this. I need to know why my father died. I have to know the truth."

"What if you disappear?" she cries. "Do you know what that would do to me? I love you." Her pain hurts me, but her fear doesn't make me scared. I'm too far gone to be afraid anymore.

"I don't want to leave you and I don't want to disappear." I wrap my arm around her shoulders. "You're my best friend and it would kill me not to be with you, but I don't have a choice. There is no going back for me. I have to know what is happening."

"No, you don't," Lena sighs angrily. "You can forget all this and move on. That's my favorite choice."

"It's not that simple." I offer a weak smile. "I don't think I'm built that way."

"Sometimes it feels like I don't even know who you are anymore." She draws in a ragged breath. I agree with her even though I don't speak the words aloud.

"Promise me something, will you?" Lena asks as she looks back to the shore. The wall that wraps around the earth is all we can see in great detail now, but soon the city will come into view.

"Anything," I respond. "Just don't ask me to leave this alone."

"I won't ask you to do that." She shakes her head. "You've always been stubborn. Never this reckless, but always hardheaded. I wouldn't expect you to give this up. Just promise me you won't drag Tordon into this with you. I think I really like him and he's vulnerable right now. I don't want him to get hurt."

I chuckle as I lean back against the bulkhead. "My how the tides have changed."

"Shut up," Lena laughs. "And promise me you'll be careful."

"I'll do my best," I reassure her. That's all any of us can promise anyway.

*

The giant stands on the docks waiting for us as we pull into the harbor. His massive arms are folded across his bare chest. Now that I think of it, I've never even seen him wear a shirt in winter.

"Hey Tordon," Lena calls out. "I think your father is upset."

"Curse the gods," Tordon spits as he eases the boat into her spot.

"What were you thinking, boy?" Aegir's voice booms through the weekend silence of the fishing docks.

"I just wanted to take the girls out for a ride." Tordon stands toe to toe with his father as he holds out a hand to help Lena down from the steps.

"And the girls wanted to see the fuel station?" Aegir's voice drops low, but the baritone rumbles against my skin.

"How do you know that's where I went?" Tordon doesn't flinch. I'd have flinched standing in front of his father like that.

"Never mind that," Aegir spits through clenched teeth. "Go home. I'll meet you there."

"I'll see you later." Lena waves goodbye as she hurries away.

"And you." Aegir turns to face me. I freeze on the dock. "You, little Brooke, will meet me here tomorrow to work off the debt of fuel you spent."

"No, dad." Tordon steps in front of me, giving a moment of reprieve so I can catch my breath. "It wasn't Brooke's idea. She didn't want to run the engine. It was my fault and I'll pay it back."

"Go home," Aegir commands. Tordon hesitates. He's trying to protect me, but I can't let him suffer if there's a way to help. I step out from behind his back.

"You will be here tomorrow at sunrise and help me run the nets all day." Aegir's face is red. I've never had his anger directed at me before and I do my best to stand strong in the force of it.

"Aye sir," I say weakly as I raise my chin. "I'll let Gertrude know and be here in the morning."

"She already knows," Aegir growls. My heartrate quickens. He stares intently in my eyes, willing me to look at him, and gives me the subtlest of winks. Tordon sees it too. There's no other reason he'd back down this easily.

"I'm sorry father," he hangs his head.

"I'm sorry too," I add respectfully.

"Go on now." Aegir nods. "You'll be here in the morning to work off your debt."

I don't say anything else as I hurry up the docks. Whatever Aegir wants to tell me will be out on the open sea away from listening ears.

.

☦ CHAPTER SIX ☦

I still have the rest of the evening to myself. Lena and Tordon must already be safe at home with their families. I wander the wharf aimlessly as my thoughts keep me company. There's a trinket stall tucked between the fish markets. I haven't been to it since I was a little girl, but I find myself drawn to it now.

Bits of chipped pottery, corroded brass compacts and doorknobs, and sea glass pendants twisted with aluminum wire all adorn the table in front of me.

"Are you looking for anything in particular?" The woman shopkeeper has her hair tied back in leather strips exposing her high cheekbones and beautiful face.

"A gift for a child." I smile at her but she doesn't smile back.

"How about this?" She points to a set of plastic dice. When she speaks, I see her teeth are rotten and black. I quickly direct my gaze to where she points. A little tin cup with a small boat etched on it holds smooth colored marbles. The glitter of one catches the setting rays of the sun and reflects it back to me.

The marble reminds me of the stone that Zander tried to take from the wall. He hasn't been back there in a few days, not since I slipped from the wharf while holding him in my arms. I cringe with shame and regret at the memory. *How could I be so careless?*

Maybe that is what I'm doing right now. If asking questions is wrong and could get me in trouble, will I accidently take someone else down with me? The watchmen are here for a reason. What would happen to the earth without them?

Overcrowding is what they call it. Too little land and too many people fighting over too few resources. Life on the sea is hard. We battle the elements and fight to survive. The work never ends. What would people do if the wall was left unguarded? Would they rush the gates and force their way in? The retirees couldn't hold them back. Could we regulate ourselves? No one I know seems to think so. Maybe the watchmen are corrupt, but who am I to question their methods? They've been protecting the earth for longer than I've been alive.

"Are you going to buy something?" the shopkeeper sighs impatiently.

"I'll take the marbles," I quickly respond. "Thank you."

*

"Auntie Brookie," Zander squeals as I open the door to Meghan's house. I hand him the cup and he studies it in amazement. "Are those for me?"

"Make sure you keep them away from your sister." I ruffle his curly brown. "Especially when she starts to crawl. You don't want her to eat one."

"I will." Zander nods solemnly as he inspects the gift. "Look at the ship here! It's just like the one I offered the gods."

"It sure is sweetie." I smile. "I think it's a sign that the gods are watching over you." He beams as he sits on the floor and begins to remove each marble to hold it up to the light.

Meghan and Rowan are sitting at the table picking crabmeat from shells.

"What did you do today?" I take the seat beside my sister and reach into the pot for a crab.

"You're looking at it." Meghan arches her back and rubs a fist against her spine. "The watchmen placed a large order."

"Of picked crabmeat?" I ask incredulously. "Why couldn't they pick it themselves?"

"I don't know." Meghan shrugs. "I'm not complaining though. They're paying us for it."

Rowan is silent as he methodically breaks the shell with his bare hands and then gently frees the meat from the carcass. He's always quiet. It normally wouldn't bother me, but then again, he normally at least acknowledges that I am here.

"Did I interrupt something?" I ask them both.

"No." Meghan shakes her head. "Rowan was just admitting he was wrong." Rowan says nothing as he breaks the Dungeness crab in half.

"It doesn't sound like he is admitting anything," I chuckle. The faintest hint of a smile curls his lips.

"This conversation is over." Meghan sweeps the discarded shells from the table into the full bucket and carries it outside.

"Do I want to know what's going on?" I quietly ask my brother-in-law. He shakes his head.

"You already do know." Meghan rolls her eyes as she rejoins us at the table. "It's your fault too."

"My fault?" I ask wide-eyed. "I just got here."

"It's your stupid questions," Meghan groans. "All this talk of not trusting the watchmen. Now Rowan thinks he agrees with you, but he is wrong and he knows it."

"I didn't say I agree with her," Rowan's deep voice rumbles softly. "I just said she might be right. None of us trust the watchmen and the way they handle things is questionable. She's justified in asking questions." I bite my lip to hide my smile.

"It's not funny." Meghan glares at me. "It's stupid and dangerous. What would we do if you disappeared?"

Rowan lowers his head. "I would never be that reckless."

"Then why are we even talking like this when it will only bring trouble?" She narrows her eyes at her husband. Rowan stays silent. "Like I said, he was just admitting he was wrong."

*

Rowan shoulders the pails of picked crabmeat and leaves to take them to the docks. The ferry that carries watchmen and supplies back and forth to their ship is waiting. Our harbor is too shallow for the large ship to enter. I imagine most harbors are like this. The sea is deeper the further out you go, but it's so unbelievably vast that you need a large carrier like the watchmen live on just to navigate it.

I offer to walk with Rowan, but Meghan insists I stay longer. She makes an excuse of needing help with Zander and Thora while she cooks, but I can tell she just doesn't want me speaking with Rowan alone. It's kind of funny. I've never been considered a bad influence before.

"Are you okay?" Meghan asks as I sit on the floor building block towers with Zander.

"Why wouldn't I be?" I pause, mid-stack, to look at her.

"No," she sighs. "I mean, are you really okay? Do you feel normal? Are you having crazy thoughts you can't control?" I study her face for any trace of humor. There isn't any.

"Everything I think is crazy lately, but I can control it." I shrug. "I think I'm okay. Maybe not normal though. A week ago, I felt like a different person, but I like the person I'm becoming."

"I don't." My sister shakes her head. "I knew when you got out of that house and away from mother that the freedom would hit you hard. But I expected you to party, maybe get a boyfriend, not try to disappear."

"I'm not trying to disappear," I explain. "I just want to know the truth. I want to know why dad died. I want to know what the watchmen are lying about." Meghan drops the spatula in the sink and holds her arms out to me.

"Come here," she demands. I do as I'm told. She squeezes me tightly and sighs against my shoulder. "You know I love you right?"

"I love you too," I laugh. "You've always been there for me. I wish I didn't worry you."

"I'm always going to worry." She holds me close and for a moment it feels like I'm a little girl again. Despite her flaws, I'm proud she is my sister. "I'm a mother. That's what we do."

"No, that's what good mothers do and you're a good mom." I lean back so I can look her in the eyes. "But you're also a terrible cook. The kelp is burning."

"Shit," Meghan screams as she attempts to salvage the meal. I leave before Rowan returns. The sun has already set and I want to get a good night's sleep before whatever torture awaits me with Aegir tomorrow.

*

A tidal wave is coming. The pressure in the air builds sending tingling currents down my skin and sucking the oxygen from my lungs. I force myself to look away from the receding water and turn to scream. The sirens haven't sound. I need to let everyone know, but when I turn there is nothing behind me. There's no one to warn.

It's only me left alone with the raging sea and my back against the wall that towers toward the brackish blue sky. The water reaches up, baring her chest to the wall. This display isn't for me. There is some kind of war between the strength of the ocean and that of the rusted iron that protects the earth.

I'm just caught in the middle. There is nothing I can do but stand tall in the face of the sea and all her glory. Maybe I am the wall, trying my hardest to protect the hidden treasures behind me, but I am also the sea. I want her to know this.

I wish the pounding of my heart would be louder than the waves just long enough for her to hear that I am alive. That I exist. That I need her to survive.

The wave reaches its full height. The water clears momentarily as it mixes with the air. In that moment I see all the trinkets of a long-forgotten world. Plastic bags, corroded metal, shells of picked through crabs- they all rise up with the wave. Their sea burial is not final.

I take in the sight of all this in slow motion. There's nowhere for me to run. The wall blocks my only escape. I'll be swept away with the rest of the world when the sea unleashes her fury.

Except, I don't want to go. My heart races as I struggle to formulate a plan in the face of this. I can't go down silently. I want to fight. I race to the wall as the wave descends. My feet dig into the wet sand and I beat my fist against the rusted metal. I'd tear it down if I could, but I'm not strong enough. And I'm not as strong as the ocean.

I turn to her in the moments before the wave crashes around me. I don't cry. I don't beg. My heart hardens with a singular focus as I watch the water littered with the remnants of the past crash down around me.

*

I wake in a cold sweat not fully rested from my awful nightmare. The dawn hasn't yet peaked, but I hurry to wash my face from the terror I experienced during the night. It's cold in my room. I slip my arms into the sleeves of my father's jacket and hold it close around me. Then I quietly make my way out of the tavern and head to the fishing docks.

*

"Just on time," Aegir states as he walks toward the *Bara*. I've been waiting for over an hour for him to show up. The other fishermen begin to filter onto the docks, yawning and grunting to one another in the early morning language. Aegir climbs onto the boat and drops his crate of bait.

"Are you coming?" The giant leans over the rail and eyes me warily. I shiver beneath my father's coat, completely mystified as to how Aegir can withstand this cold without a shirt.

"Who else are we waiting for?" I ask as I climb the steps.

"It's just us today." His deep voice booms over the roaring start of the engine. He doesn't even pretend to set the sails. I cast a worried glance to the docks and see Tordon standing there with an encouraging smile on his face, but he doesn't look convinced that everything will be okay.

Gray mist and fog rolls across the sea. The moon still peeks through the clouds even as the sun's rays begin to lighten the sky. I yawn and a fit of chills racks my body.

"Drop the line six meters," Aegir commands as he kills the engine and raises the sails. The *Bara* bobs on the open stretch of water. In the distance are more fishing boats each staying to their own course and avoiding one another in a dance of trailing fishing lines and nets. It's fascinating to see how delicate these hardened men and women are with their craft.

We had a family boat when I was younger. My father would take us out to teach us how to fish, but he was more suited to fixing and building things. Somedays I wonder what exactly it is I'm suited for. The boat lurches as the line snags the first fish of the day.

"Hold the helm," Aegir calls. I rush to take his place at the wheel. He laughs such a deep chested menacing sound that it seems to come from the depths of the ocean as he fights against the line. The tension of the line gives and then tightens testing the strength of the giant's muscles. I gasp and let go of the wheel when he is suddenly pulled forward over the railing.

"I said hold her steady," Aegir laughs as he leans back and singlehandedly lifts a tuna onto the boat. The beast of a fish is easily as tall as Zander and thrashes around the deck until Aegir leans down to slice its throat.

"Alright." He smiles as he stows the fish in the well. "Get the line again."

By midmorning I'm sweating and covered in the pungent smell of fish and bait. My father's jacket is stored safely below deck. I'm glad I no longer need it. As it stands, I'll have to burn the clothes I'm wearing if I ever hope to get the stench out.

Aegir is mostly silent, only calling out orders when needed. He doesn't need me here. I'm certain he could do this all by himself. I wait patiently for the real reason to emerge for my required presence. He's either enjoying making me suffer or waiting for the right time to speak. Whatever the reason, I know better than to rush the giant.

The action slows around midday. Aegir pulls out a pail of food and hands it to me. Gratefully, I accept. The dried jerky in my jacket pocket doesn't smell as appetizing as this.

Aegir carries out a second pail and drops anchor before sitting on the bench with his back against the rail. He chews silently, watching the sea stretched out around us and letting the sun warm his chest. My cheeks and lips are wind burnt. It's difficult to fully open my mouth. I break off small pieces of the seaweed wrapped fish and savor every tiny bite.

"I've always liked you Brooke," Aegir says ending the silence of our meal. "And I always thought you'd make a good match for Tordon."

I choke on a bit of fish and swallow hard. *Is this what he brought me here to talk about?*

"It doesn't seem like that will be happening anytime soon," he continues, ignoring my look of stunned surprise. "But I'll never give up hope."

I feel my cheeks flush under the newly reddened and dried skin. "Aegir, I…"

He holds up a hand to silence me. "That's not why I brought you out here today."

"Okay." I set the pail down beside my feet. "Why did you bring me out here?"

"Do you think you are the first person in the history of our world to ask these questions?" His sharp eyes turn to me demanding a response.

"Honestly?" I chew the inside of my cheek. "I don't know, but no one is asking them now. No one seems to care."

"When your father and I were younger, a few years older than you are now, we did some stupid things. We thought some stupid things. When Tordon came to me with your plan to get rid of the watchmen I almost laughed. That was my and your father's plan." Aegir smiles at the memory.

"Then why didn't you do it?" I stare at him in wonder. He's never not followed through with something.

"Because it was a foolish plan." His smile fades as quickly as it came. "If Henry hadn't talked some sense into us then I wouldn't be standing here today."

"My father knew Henry?" I ask.

"A few of us do." Aegir nods.

"But he told Thomas he'd hired a drifter." The puzzle in my head smashes into pieces as I try to process this.

"Henry is a drifter," Aegir chuckles. "Among many other things."

"If you are so fond of this person," I say. "Then tell me why he killed my father."

"That's why you are fixated on this." Aegir leans forward and places his forearms on top of his knees as he studies me. "This makes more sense. You never were a rebellious one. I wondered where this started."

"It started with the fact that we are being lied to." I glare at him. "Jillian is gone. My father is dead. The watchmen took his paintings from me."

"I see," Aegir sighs. "You are fueled by revenge."

"No." I shake my head. "I'm fueled by the desire to know the truth. Why do we let the watchmen treat us this way? Why don't we do anything to stop them?"

"It's not as simple as it seems." He runs his fingers through his beard and suddenly looks so much older, as if the weight of the world were on his shoulders.

My heart aches for him. "They had something to do with Endre's death too, didn't they?"

He blinks back the truth and doesn't respond. It's alright. I already know what the answer is.

"Never mind that," he says softly. "Why don't you tell me what you think you know? You want answers and I'll do my best to give them to you."

I bite my cracked lip and turn to stare at the sun's rays glittering on top of the water. The rocking of the boat is calming unlike the current that runs through my mind.

"I haven't been able to piece it all together," I answer. "The watchmen don't care for us. They treat us like we are beneath them. People disappear for no reason. Everyone is afraid to speak out against them. I feel like they are hiding something from us."

"Everything you speak is the truth," Aegir remarks. "The way they are trained gives them an air of superiority. Their methods are questionable, but their job is a hard one."

"Why aren't they honest?" I turn to look at him. "Why can't we question what they do?"

"Power lies in obedience," Aegir explains. "Did you ever question your father when he made the rules?" I think of Meghan and me protesting against learning how to read.

"All the time," I smirk. "But my father was a good and fair man. We weren't punished for speaking our mind."

"Imagine if everyone spoke like that to the watchmen. Questioning their methods and protesting against them diminishes their control. What would become of the wall if they weren't strong enough to protect it?"

"Okay," I sigh in frustration. "But that still doesn't explain my father's death."

"Your father drowned," Aegir answers quietly. I want to scream at him, to pull whatever truths he is hiding from his head and force him to be honest with me.

"That's a lie and you know it." I stand and fold my arms over my chest. "He was killed for his machine. Jillian was taken for her growing system. It all has something to do with Henry and the plans for the invention."

"Calm down, child." Aegir cleans up the remains of his lunch and stores them back in his pail. "If Henry was in contact with either of them, I can assure you he was only trying to help."

"Fat lot of good that did either of them," I mutter through clenched teeth. "Why would the watchmen consider them a threat? They both only wanted to make our world better."

Aegir stands. "In our world, strength is better than intelligence."

"So, my father was killed for being smart." I arch an eyebrow.

"No," he grumbles. "Your father died from being careless."

"Was Endre careless too?" I spit. His eyes flash with an anger so intense that I take a step backwards.

"No," he says bitterly. "Endre died because I was careless. I shouldn't have let him go fishing alone at night."

I should stop, I'm pressing him too far, but I can't until I know more. "What is your relationship with the watchmen? How do you proclaim to know so much about them?"

"I have no relationship with them." He narrows his eyes and his voice lowers into the sound that makes grown men cringe. "I do what I have to in order to take care of my family and survive. Hear me now girl, I am telling you to do the same."

I want to cry, but I don't. Instead, I force myself to stand steady against the weight of his warning. "I respect you Aegir, but I don't think I can stop until I learn the whole truth. Will Henry speak with me?"

Aegir's eyes open wide in surprise. I don't think he was expecting his plan to silence me not to work. "At the rate you are going, he might have to." He places the lunch pail below deck. "But I'm not sure if he will or not."

"What's that supposed to mean?" I follow him to the helm.

"Nothing," he says as he pulls up the anchor. "You are more stubborn than I gave you credit for is all. I don't think there is anything I can say that will make you stop." There's a hint of pride in his annoyance.

I cling to that even if it's foolish. "I don't want you to hate me. I just want to know why my father died and why they took the plans from me. Why can't his machine work?"

"Those answers I can't give you." Aegir holds the wheel steady as he turns the boat around. "But I do ask that if you continue on this path, that you leave Tordon out of it. I've already lost one son. I can't bear to lose another."

The wind picks up the open sails, propelling us forward and quieting any further conversation. I force myself to keep working through the rest of the afternoon despite the blisters forming on my palms from the plastic netting. Aegir doesn't let me rest anyway.

It's good to stay busy now. The work helps slow down my racing thoughts and lets me focus on coherent ones. Aegir's words weigh heavily on my heart. If I'm going to get in trouble for questioning the watchmen, then I need to make sure no one else is brought down with me. I love them too much to see anyone get hurt. With that decided, there is only one thing left for me to do. I need to find a way to speak with Henry.

☦ CHAPTER SEVEN ☦

"Why are we heading back so early?" I call over the wind. The wall and the shoreline grow larger before me. The sun is still high in the sky and the other boats are distant rocks in the ocean as they continue fishing for the day.

"Don't you have work to do?" Aegir chuckles.

I stare at him in shock. "I assumed that you spoke with the spinners."

"You assumed wrong." He pinches his lips together in a tight line, but he can't hide the amusement that lights up his crystal blue eyes.

Curse this man. I race below deck to grab my father's jacket and reemerge just as Aegir pulls us into the harbor. I don't wait for him to dock. Instead, I leap from the bow onto the rusted planks before the *Bara* is nestled in her resting place. Aegir's deep chested laugh taunts me as I run through the city toward the caves where the spinners sit.

*

"Where have you been?" Lena asks. "And why do you smell so bad?"

"I was with Aegir," I groan. "I didn't know I'd have to work tonight."

"You seem to not know a lot of things lately," she says sadly.

"But I'm trying to figure them out," I answer playfully, hoping to ease the tension.

"Whatever," she whispers. It's so unlike her that I'm stunned into silence.

My hands shake as I grip the plastic strip. Three twists and a turn. It was always so easy before, but now my palms are blistered from the day spent fishing and this simple movement hurts. I struggle to tie the knot. Margaret gives me a sympathetic smile and I work harder to not let the pain show. Lena's back tightens behind me.

"What is it?" I ask. The exhaustion from the day catches up with me all at once. I don't want to play these games right now.

"Nothing." Lena continues with her work.

I let the plastic strip I'm holding fall to the rock. I'm so tired that I can't think straight. Lena is mad at me. I want to know why.

"Tell me," I demand. I feel her rage boil inside her without even seeing her face. It's a tempest brewing, a tidal wave building, the rising pressure before a coming storm. A lifetime ago this might have worried me, but I'm too exhausted to care.

"You are acting crazy," Lena exclaims. "My mother is worried. She's right too. We never expected this from you."

"What did you expect?" My voice comes with a level of exhaustion I didn't know I was capable of.

"Not this," she says softly.

"What did your mother say that is making you act this way?" I ask. "You are confusing me."

I glance up at the wharf. A lone watchman passes by. He doesn't stop, but his gait is slow enough that he can listen if he wants to.

Lena watches him go. "My mother is heartbroken," she whispers. "She thinks it would be better if I stayed away from you for a while."

I force myself to pick up the plastic and twist it between my fingers. "Your mother is right," I say. "I refuse to be the reason for anyone else to get hurt. This is my path. I don't need anyone else on it with me."

"Brooke," Lena cries out in a panic. "I don't want anything to happen to you either."

"And I don't want anything to happen to you," I sigh heavily as I lean forward on the rock, not trusting Lena to support my back. "That's why I'm doing this alone."

"I'm sorry," Lena whispers.

"I'm sorry too," I mutter.

*

I'm the first to stand when the sun sets and the first to stow away my bag of plastic strips. I don't wait for Lena, and she doesn't hurry to catch up with me. In all our years as friends I've come to think of Beau as a second mother, but maybe I was wrong. I don't blame her though. She just wants to protect her daughters. I didn't realize I'd ever be someone that you'd need protecting from.

All I want to do is sleep. I hurry across the docks to the wharf where the lanterns are being lit for the night. It's the same thing that always happens, but everything seems different now. *How can the whole world change in just a few days?*

I don't notice him standing in the shadows of the walkways until I almost collide into his chest.

"What are you doing?" I cry out in surprise. "Are you watching me again?"

"Should I be?" Calder's tone is threatening, a silent warning. It takes everything in me not to scream.

"Get out of my way." I return his glare with one of my own. "I have nothing left for you to take from me."

"What is that supposed to mean?" He sounds genuinely confused.

"Nothing," I sigh stepping past him. "I'm just exhausted. I don't want to talk to you right now."

He silently returns to whatever it is that he was actually watching. I turn to look in the direction he stares but struggle to see anything in the darkness.

"I thought you were leaving," he states without looking at me.

"I am." My feet don't move. Silence hangs in the air between us.

"Listen," I muster the courage to say. "You are the last person on earth that I want to ask for help from."

"Then don't," he responds coldly.

"I wouldn't if I wasn't out of options." I roll my eyes. "But I need to speak with Henry. Just one conversation, that's all I want. Is there a way that I can get in touch with him?"

"Didn't I tell you to leave this alone?" His exasperation infuriates me.

"You have no right to tell me what to do." I glare at him.

"Actually, I do." He takes a step forward closing the distance between us and forcing me to look up at his face. "If I give you an official order, you have no choice but to obey."

"Or what?" I stand my ground. "You'll make me disappear? Get it through that thick skull of yours, I don't care if I disappear. I want to know why my father died and I'm not stopping until I have the truth."

He smirks at me. "You stupid girl. I know you don't care for your own life, but what about the lives of those you love?"

"I loved my father," I say. "Does his life not matter?" I stare into his dark brown eyes. They almost look black in the shadows. The only sound comes from our breathing as our chests rise and fall.

"Go home." Calder steps away. "And pray to your gods that you never have to meet Henry."

"Why is that?" I cross my arms and refuse to move. "It seems that most people think he is a nice guy."

"He is," Calder chuckles. "If you are worth something."

The insult stings. It reminds me of my mother and all the times she assured me that I wasn't important. But I'm not a child anymore.

"If I'm not worth anything, why not get rid of me and be done with it?" I ask.

"Don't tempt me." It's the first real smile I've ever seen on his face. The way his eyes light up is unnerving. He almost looks kind.

"Fine." I clench my teeth. "If you won't help me then I'll find another way."

The humor quickly fades from his face. "No, you won't. If you don't leave this alone, not only will you disappear, but I'll take your family too."

His words punch me in the stomach harder than any hit I've ever taken. Tears well in my eyes as my breath escapes my lungs in a single gasp.

"You can't do that," I stammer. "They are not a part of this."

"Guilty by association." He shrugs.

"Our neighbors won't stand for it. Meghan and Rowan are good. They have children." As soon as the words leave my mouth, I know they are nothing but a lie. No one will say anything.

"Maybe it will seem like an accident." The muscles in his jaw tighten as he turns to look away. I feel like I'm going to be sick.

"I hate you." Tears burn a path down my cheeks.

"Go home now," he demands. "And do as I say this time."

*

"Are you planning to wake up today?" Zoe's voice is punctuated by the incessant knocking on my door. I bury my face under the blanket and groan.

There isn't a single part of me that wants to get out of this bed.

"I tried," Zoe calls out in frustration as she stomps down the walkway. I force myself to sit up, knowing that it'll be Gertrude who comes next and I don't have the energy for whatever work she'll give me for being late to the morning shift.

The paper with the copy of my father's plans sits unfolded on the bedside table. I stare at it in defeat as the memory of Calder's words brings a fresh wave of pain. I failed before I even got started. *I'm so sorry dad.*

My feet are heavy as I force them to move across the bedroom floor. With blistered hands from Aegir's fishing expedition, I turn the knob and open the door. Gertrude is just now reaching the top step. She gives me a long look before her face softens.

"Are you sick?" she asks gravely.

"No," I whisper. "Just tired."

"Well, figure out a way to wake up." She turns to leave. "The customers will be here soon."

*

My stomach groans in protest as I refuse the plate of food Rupert offers. Thankfully, he doesn't relent. I don't want to eat. I just want to sleep, but my body betrays me and scarfs down the food anyway. Survival is funny like that.

My meager tips attest to the fact that it hurts to smile. It hurts to do anything but sleep. I want to go back to my bed.

"What's wrong with you?" Zoe asks as we wipe down the tables after the customers leave. I don't respond.

"Fine." She shrugs. "Stay silent if you want. You can do the dishes."

Tears roll down my face despite my best efforts to keep them in. I don't hate Zoe, but she's not exactly the kind of person that you share your secrets with. The side of her I only ever see with her daughter comes out as she awkwardly tries to hug me.

"Gods," she sighs. "Don't break down like this. I'll do the dishes. Just tell me what is wrong."

"I can't." The words get stuck in my throat and I cough to clear it. "No one else can get caught up in this with me."

"Is this about Calder?" She steps back and eyes me from head to foot.

"Sort of." I struggle to put myself back together. "I really hate that guy."

Zoe's laugh is short and fleeting. "Are you sure you hate him?"

"Yes." The blood drains from my face. "Why wouldn't I?"

"No reason." She bends to wipe down a chair. "I'm just not sure that he hates you that much."

Now I'm laughing. "Trust me, he hates me just as much as I hate him."

Zoe pauses, twisting the rag between her fingers, and stares at me intently. Whatever she hopes to find isn't there. "I heard the watchmen talking. They said he risked something for you."

"Risked what?" *Gods I'm confused.* "I'm telling you; he hates me."

"You know, not all the watchmen are bad." She drops the rag into the bucket and sits on the chair she just wiped down.

"Could have fooled me." I dunk my own rag and resume cleaning.

"I'm serious." She lowers her voice to a whisper. "I've never talked about this to anyone, but I'm sure some people have figured it out. I wouldn't even tell you. Except, I think you need to hear this. Iris's father was a watchman and we loved each other. He had to leave us, but I will always love him."

"What?" My jaw drops to the floor. I toss my rag into the bucket and sit on the chair beside her. "I had no clue. Where is he now?"

Zoe closes her eyes. When she opens them again there is only the distant look I've come to know so well. "He's dead. There was an uprising at the

Cortez gate and he fought to keep the peace. He had one final tour and then he was coming back to us. Now he'll never get the chance."

My heart shatters into a million pieces. I reach for her hand, but she jerks it away. "I don't need your sympathy. I only want you to understand that the world isn't as black and white as it seems to you."

I swallow down my pity and try not to show it in my eyes. Zoe is so much stronger than I ever could have imagined. I want to ask her more questions, but her love for the watchmen is written plainly on her arms. She won't speak badly about them.

"Okay," I say softly. "I'll do the dishes today."

She rises from the chair and gives me a playful wink. "That was my plan all along. I knew it would work."

*

I should go see Meghan before my shift with the spinners, but I can't bear to look at her right now. I'm ashamed at how close I came to putting her in danger. The guilt nags at me until all I want to do is sleep. I take a nap, a gloriously dreamless nap, and when I wake, I stare at my mural. I think I'll paint some more tonight.

I waste the rest of the afternoon walking the docks and the main wharf trying to recapture the joy I used to feel in this city. I purposefully avoid Jillian's shop, Bergah's stall, and my childhood home, but I force myself to really look at everything else I pass.

How foolish was I to question our way of life? Sure, it's rough, but look at the way people work and live in harmony. Survival is its own kind of painting of colors all working and bleeding together to produce the end result. What if the answers changed all of this? What if someone I loved got hurt? I'd be no better than my mother. The squid ink would be on my hands and I'd ruin this painting for everyone.

I arrive at the rocks early and pull out the bags of plastic for all the spinners. Today seems like the perfect day to be a little less selfish. Margaret arrives just as I finish setting up.

"Did you find your answers?" Her eyes sparkle mischievously.

"I found enough to know that I don't need to look anymore." I'm not sure why I lower my head in shame, but I do it anyway. More of the spinners arrive saving me from further conversation. I join in singing the songs with the truest part of my heart.

The rock I sit on feels cold despite my earnest attempt at setting things right. I need to apologize to so many people. All evening I scan the docks waiting for my best friend. The sun dips behind the horizon and Lena still hasn't come to work. Worry tugs at my insides as I walk to the tavern. *Would she really be so mad at me as to skip a shift with the spinners?*

It's not until I walk through the kitchen door and see her carrying a tray of food that the tension eases from my shoulders. We lock eyes but she doesn't return my smile. She has every right not to. I've been so caught up in my own world lately that I forgot what her schedule looks like.

"Did you need any help tonight?" I ask hopefully. Maybe I can make things up to her this way.

"We're not busy," Lena responds as she pushes open the door to the dining room.

"I'm really sorry." I lower my face. Lena pauses and tears form in her eyes making them shine in the lantern light.

"It's okay," she whispers. "I'll come to your room when my shift is over and we can talk."

"Alright." I nod. I want to hug her but her arms are full and I don't want to knock over the tray. I'm not sure if she has forgiven me. It's a start though. Rupert hands me some crab cakes and I carry them up the stairs.

It'll be a few hours until the night shift is done. I sit on the edge of my bed and stare at the blank space on my mural. The ship at sea, the raging storm, and my self portrait all mix in a blur of frustrated tears. I use the sleeve of my father's jacket to dry my eyes and then shrug my arms free from it.

I am not my father. Nor am I my mother. Nothing I can do is worth more than my sister's safety. I paint her face. The freckles on her cheeks are my grandmother's freckles. I have a few, but not as many as she does. Her eyes are a little too large. It helps to capture the emotions within them.

I paint Rowan. His eyes are trained on my sister's face and his bushy beard only partially hides his quiet smile. Thora's face is screaming red. The perfect representation of the night I met her. Zander's eyes are large too. Just like his mother. He holds Meghan's hand and grins at me from ear to ear.

I paint Lena. It's hard to get a perfect likeness, but I swirl her long black hair like seaweed as it wraps around Tordon. His fingers tangle in it. I give them both lovers' smiles and eyes for each other. Zoe's bird boned face and tiny nose stretch into delicate arms that scoop up a chubby little girl. As I outline the giant's chin, Aegir's form taking shape beneath my brush, I hear it again.

The music drifts softly through the tavern, loud enough to be heard over the other noises, and delicately makes its way to my room. Calder is playing his guitar.

The paintbrush drips in my hand. I use the worn strips of leather to blot it so it doesn't drip on the floor as I walk across the room. I crack the door open to better hear the sound. It's amazing how such an oddly shaped box can produce this vibrant music.

Just like the first time I heard it, I feel each note dance across my skin and raise the hairs on the back of my neck. The music is beautiful. Too bad the musician is so nasty. I don't mean to linger in the doorway as long as I do. When I look up, Calder is watching me while his fingers strum the instrument. A wave of anger makes me shudder and I move to slam the door shut, but Lena's strained face catches my attention.

She's serving the watchmen drinks. Her usually calm and playful confidence is replaced with a tight-lipped smile. Drake whispers something in her ear and her face pales. She tries to walk away, but he puts an arm around her waist holding her back.

I throw the brushes into the wash basin and race out of the room to help my friend. She breaks free and starts running down the opposite staircase. Drake follows closely behind. Fear forces me into action. I take the steps two at a time on the staircase closest to me hoping to cut him off at the bottom and allow her time to escape.

The music stops playing and the other watchmen lean over the banister watching the show. Either the customers in the tavern haven't noticed or they are pretending not to see. The thought disgusts me, but I can't do anything about that anymore. All I can do is help my friend.

Lena and Drake aren't on the stairs as I reach the tavern floor. I wildly scan the room and see the watchman's broad back with the green uniform stretched across it as he enters the kitchen. I catch the door just before it swings shut.

"This is your boyfriend?" Drake laughs. Tordon stacks a keg of beer on top of the other and turns in confusion just in time to catch Lena as she flings herself into his arms.

"You can't be in here," I say sidestepping Drake's back and planting myself firmly in front of him.

"I just wanted to see." Drake smiles playfully before lowering his face so that it's inches from mine. "Plus, you don't give me orders. Scurry back to your room before you get in trouble." He pushes me to the side.

I cast a worried glance to Rupert. He busies himself with cooking and doesn't acknowledge we are here. Tordon moves Lena behind him, pushing her outside into the night past the open kitchen door.

"I'm not done speaking with you yet, Lena." Drake grins revealing a set of perfectly white teeth. "Why don't you stick around and explain to me how a week ago you were leading me on like a filthy wharf slut and now you suddenly have this sorry excuse for a boyfriend?"

Tordon's face goes red as his fists clench at his side. Lena cries as she tries to pull him out of the door with her, but Tordon doesn't budge. He's not going to. I've seen him mad, but never this visibly angry. He's going to attack a watchman. My heart beats hard against my ribcage. *Tordon is going to disappear.*

"I think you should leave now." I push myself between the two men and stop them both from advancing. "You said what you wanted to say. It's time to go back to your friends."

Drake ignores me and moves his still smiling face over my shoulder. His arms hang limply at his side. I realize what he is doing even though Tordon can't see it in his blinding rage.

"Tordon." I turn and scream in his face. "He wants you to hit him. Stop!"

Tordon blinks, pausing just long enough for my shoving and Lena's pulling to get him outside the door. I slam it shut and block Drake from following them. The smile never leaves his mouth and he leans forward until his breath is hot against me.

"You are all ocean scum," he whispers. I raise my hand and slap my palm as hard as I can across his cheek.

It instantly burns, stinging my skin, and I pull it quickly away as the horror sinks in. A raising red perfect outline of my fingers lingers on his face. His eyes widen as he looks at me.

"What are you doing, man?" Calder's hand is on Drake's shoulder pulling him away. Both men stare at each other. A low chuckle escapes from Drake's lips breaking their tension.

"Your little pet's time is up." He gently touches the welt on his cheek. I stand against the door shaking and holding the offending hand that betrayed me away from my body.

"I didn't mean to," I stutter. "He was provoking Tordon and called Lena names. Then he was in my face and I... I didn't mean to."

"Of course you didn't." Drake shakes his head. "None of you barbarians can control yourselves. You're all feral and irrational. Just like your slut friend."

My hand drops to my side and I raise my chin. Pride for my action suddenly fills me. I only wish it would have been worse.

"Go to your room," Calder commands as he leads Drake out of the kitchen. I slump against the door as the full weight of what I've just done comes crashing down on my head.

"I think you should do as he says," Rupert whispers softly as he turns the whale steaks to keep them from burning in their own fat.

"You saw what happened!" Outrage makes my voice squeak embarrassingly high. "How could you just stand there and do nothing?"

"I value my life," he explains. "My family depends on me."

"It doesn't have to be this way." Now that the adrenaline begins to fade, tears spring to my eyes and I angrily wipe my blistered and bruising hand across them.

"It's always been this way," he says. "Go do as the watchman told you. I'll let Gertrude know what happened."

In my room, panic sets in. I need to tell Meghan I'm sorry and tell Zander goodbye, but I shouldn't go anywhere near them right now. *Maybe I can run.* Running sounds like a good plan. I grab my father's bag and hastily pack everything I own. Before I secure the woven plastic bag of paints to the side, I write the words "I love you all" under the portraits I just painted.

The rest of them won't be able to read it, but Meghan will and she'll tell them what it says. Maybe she'll teach Zander one day. My heart breaks in half as I stare at their faces, but I don't have time to dwell.

How many minutes has Calder bought me? Why didn't they take me right then? Never mind that now, I have to go. Maybe I can steal a boat and sail somewhere far away. I roll up my bedding and tie it to the pack just as the heavy stomping of boots echoes across the walkway.

I'm out of time.

Tossing on my father's jacket and loading the gear on my back, I rush to the open window. There is no ledge for me to climb down safely. I'm going to have to fall onto the wharf below. The footsteps stop right outside my door. I swing one leg over the windowsill and take a deep breath to steady my nerves before swinging the other.

I cling tightly to the ledge with my arms and chest trying to give myself the shortest fall. My feet dangle in the air and the weight of the pack pulls me down. I take one last look at the door expecting them to kick it open any second. Something small slides in through the crack at the bottom and the heavy footsteps stomp away.

"Oh my gods!" a woman shrieks from the wharf below me. "That person is going to jump!"

"No, I'm not," I groan and it takes every ounce of my strength to ungracefully pull myself back up and into the room.

"Sorry about that," I call to the woman breathlessly. "It was just an accident." I give her a smile and a wave before slamming the shutters closed and locking them.

My pulse races throughout my body and my legs shake so much that I drop to my knees. I slip the bag off my shoulders and crawl across the floor to retrieve the square package that was slipped inside my room. It's paper. I press my ear against the door waiting for the sound of boots to return.

All I hear is the laughter from the customers who are completely oblivious to anything that has happened tonight. With trembling hands, I unfold the page. There's a simple message between the folds:

Meet me at the rocks tomorrow at noon.

✝ CHAPTER EIGHT ✝

I lay awake all night tossing and turning. My brain won't slow down enough to sleep. This is some kind of trick. Calder must have set it up. He's the only one I know who has paper and knows that I can read. *Unless he told the other watchmen.* Of course he told the other watchmen. They are setting this whole thing up, orchestrating it so that I walk to my own death.

I should run. But if I do, will they retaliate and hurt my sister? In my panic earlier, I hadn't thought of this. I feel so stupid. Nothing can happen to her. The kids need her to be okay.

Calder hates me. But what if he changed his mind and wants to help? Maybe he will give me some answers. *Most likely, he wants to kill me.*

I don't know what to do, but this isn't something I can ask for help with. I will be punished for hitting a watchman. Even if I'm some kind of pet or whatever Drake called me. There is no way they will let me go. I'm going to disappear. Maybe it's better to go this way. At least I know what the time will be.

In the early hours before the sun has yet risen, I sit wrapped in my father's jacket staring vacantly at the wall. No matter what is coming, I promise myself that I will face it head on.

And if today will be the day of my death, there are some things I need to do.

*

Gertrude doesn't seem to mind when I ask to leave early. The mark is burning on my forehead and I'm sure she can see it. I hug Zoe, really hug her, until I feel her relax into my arms.

"What's this about?" she asks.

"Nothing." I let her go. "You are such a strong woman. Iris is lucky to have you."

*

I knock on Lena's door. Beau answers and sleepy little girls poke their curious faces out from behind their mother's legs.

"Is Lena here?" I ask anxiously shifting from foot to foot.

"She is." Beau regards me suspiciously and I'm filled with sadness. She's never made me feel anything but loved before. "What is this about?"

"I wanted to tell her I'm sorry and that she is right." I bite my lip. "I'll stop asking questions. I don't want anyone to get hurt."

"Oh child." Beau reaches out and pulls me to her, smothering me against her chest and sobbing into my hair. "I knew you had a decent head on you."

"Ma, let her go." Lena's sighs as she reaches for my arm and drags me into the house. The younger girls clamber onto my lap as I sit on the floor in the front room. Beau returns to the kitchen giving me a warm smile as she goes.

"I was worried about you last night," Lena whispers in my ear. "Thank you for helping to get Tordon out. It took hours to calm him down and keep him from going back to find Drake. Aegir is keeping a close eye on him today."

"That's good," I whisper back even though I'm sure Beau is picking up our every word. "And I'm fine. Drake left just after you did. I'm so glad you are here for Tordon. He is going to need you."

"I don't know about that." Lena lowers her face. "He wouldn't have even been in that position if it wasn't for me."

"It wasn't your fault." I reach for her hand. "But maybe you should switch shifts for a while. Tell Gertrude to put you on the morning shift. The other girls and I can cover the nights."

"You're the best," Lena laughs. "I don't know what I would do without you."

"You'd be okay." I force myself to smile. "Besides, you've got Tordon to think about now."

*

It takes longer than I expected to pry myself from Lena's house. The sun keeps rising in the sky. I have to hurry to get to Meghan's if I am going to be on time for what might be my death. It occurs to me that being a little late won't hurt. It's probably one of the only times that I'd be okay with being late. But what if it isn't my death? What if Calder is there waiting with answers and he thinks I'm not coming? Then I won't get a chance to learn the truth before my real death which is undoubtably coming soon.

None of the watchmen standing on the wharf follow me, but every one of them I see raises his eyes when I pass. By the time I've reached my sister's house, I'm convinced I'll die on the rocks at noon and they will make it look like an accident.

It's only the smallest bit of hope, so tiny it seems like a bright red coral out of reach on the depths of the ocean floor, that keeps me moving through the door of my sister's house. It'll have to be my last stop because I won't have time to see Tordon. I hope he understands.

*

"Auntie Brookie!" Zander jumps into my arms. I swallow back the hurt that threatens to cripple me knowing this will probably be the last time I hear his little voice calling me by that name.

"Someone is going to the wall next week," Meghan laughs as she changes Thora on the floor next to Zander's scattered toys. "Maybe then I can get some more work done."

He pouts and folds his arms across his chest while pushing them out to make himself seem bigger. "I'm too old to go to the wall now."

"No, you're not." I drop down to his level. "You are the perfect age. It's time to tell you a secret anyway. This is something only grownups know. You have to go to the wall so you can learn and be smart and brave. That's the only way you will be able to get big enough to protect the earth just like we do."

"I can protect it?" His eyes widen in amazement.

"Yes. That's why you have to go. We need you on our side." I wink at my sister as Zander silently returns to his play and contemplates what I've just said.

"Good one," Meghan whispers giving me a grateful smile. "You're off early today. What do you have going on?"

"I just need to meet with someone," I answer quietly, hoping my voice won't betray my sadness.

"More questions?" she sighs.

"No more questions." I shake my head. "You were right. It's not worth putting anyone I love in danger and you can tell Rowan I said that."

"What's wrong with you?" Meghan eyes me warily. I stare at her, wanting to memorize her face. There's so much more I want to tell her. I want to thank her for always being there for me and for always caring. I want to tell her it isn't her fault that we grew up with the mother we did. I want to grab her hand and cry, beg her to run away with me. But I can't ask that of her.

"Nothing." I squeeze her in a hug before my face betrays anything. "I just want you to know I'm sorry for everything and that I love you so much."

*

The rusted metal planks support me as I walk to my certain death. I inhale deeply to calm the anxiety. *Nothing is certain.* I don't yet know what I am walking to. It's probably best not to be dramatic until certain becomes, well, certain.

The people of the city pass by me dreamlike and unaware. It's not their job to care. I lower my head as I press through the overcrowded wharf. None of these people hit a watchman. It's not their fault I'm being punished.

The docks leading to my childhood home appear in my line of vision much sooner than I'd anticipated at this trudging speed. I don't hurry now and who can blame me? Does anyone hurry to their end?

I glance up as I pass the house I grew up in. All the memories packed into metal walls where I no longer exist. I'm not sure what I hope to see. Maybe a family with children laughing through the open windows. But the storm shutters are still closed tight concealing the ghosts of our life within.

I step from the last dock onto the rocky outcropping where my father's machine once sat. *That stupid machine,* I hear my mother's voice. It was supposed to fix the earth. Instead, it left my father dead and aided me in joining him.

My eyes travel up from the treacherous rocks to face whatever calamity is about to befall me. I promised myself that I'd be brave and stare the watchmen in their eyes during my final hour.

But I'm alone. There is no crowd of men dressed in green silently swarming around me. There are only the jagged rocks, the sea, the sky, and the rapid beating of my own heart. I turn my head to the sun, letting the warm rays caress my face.

It's high noon. I'm not late to my death, though apparently everyone else is.

Carefully I walk across the rocks to the boulder overlooking the sea. I have to keep my breathing steady and force myself not to run. The anxiety of waiting feels worse than anything I've ever experienced. But I'll be good and wait here a while, sitting on my favorite spot and watching the ocean roll in while whatever is coming decides to come.

I haven't yet reached the smooth boulder when I hear music drifting up from the water. A relieving sigh deflates my lungs. Calder is here, hidden between the crevice of the rocks beneath the cliff face and strumming his guitar. My elation quickly turns to annoyance. All this build up, and for what? *But it wasn't his fault,* I remind myself. I brought this on myself.

I kneel down on the boulder and call out, "Did you want me to come down?"

He slowly removes his hand from the guitar and glares at me. "What do you think?"

I hesitate before climbing down the cliff, but whatever is about to happen is out of my control and I'd be lying if I didn't say I wasn't at least a little curious about what he has to say. Yes, I am afraid, but by gods I want to know.

"You are the dumbest person I ever met," Calder states as I step on the small portion of exposed beach beside him.

"And you are the rudest I've ever met." I let go of the last handhold on the rock and regain my footing in the sand. "What are we doing here? Is this some kind of trick?"

His face is trained on the ocean and he doesn't turn to look at me. "I don't know what I'm doing here," he says harshly. I feel like I'm being reprimanded for a crime and cold sweat forms on my palms. Maybe this was the plan all along. Calder is going to kill me and make it look like an accident.

"Okay," I say nervously. "You gave me paper with instructions. I did as you said, even though I was sure it was a trap and I was going to disappear. I'm still here. Why am I here?"

Calder half smiles but the action seems to cause him pain. "Honestly? I was hoping you were lying about being able to read."

"Only one of us is a liar." I cross my arms over my body and lean against the cliff while glaring at him. "I'm here. What do you want?" He stands silently brooding as he watches the water lap at our feet.

"Listen." The irritation crawls over my skin. "I don't know what is happening here. Am I going to be punished for smacking Drake? Are the watchmen coming for me?"

"Yes," he states. I knew that was the answer, but it's still frightening to hear it out loud.

"When?" I whisper.

"I bought you some time," he says. "Not long. A few days at most."

"Why would you do that?" I ask. Nothing about him makes sense anymore.

"I don't know." He finally turns to look at me. Mixed emotions play across his face. "I think you are probably one of the most annoying people I've ever met, but this isn't right and I don't know how to change anything. I'm hoping that doing this will help ease my conscious."

"I didn't think you had a conscious." The words are harsher than I intended them to be. Whatever he is struggling with is obviously hurting him.

"I'm sorry." I lower my voice. "I still don't understand what you are saying. What will help ease your conscious? Giving me more time? I've already said my goodbyes. Tell the watchmen they can come for me now."

"How can you not hear what I am saying?" he asks in frustration. "I'm giving you a chance."

"A chance for what?" I laugh. "To escape? I would have already run if I was going to."

"You wouldn't have been able to run. We would have stopped you." He lets out a heavy sigh. "I'm giving you a chance to talk with Henry before the watchmen come for you."

"How?" The slightest bit of hope eases the heaviness from my heart. If I could at least speak with Henry then I might be able to get some answers. Then all of this won't have been for nothing and I can go in peace.

"Did you really paint that mural in your room?" he turns away as he asks.

"Yes." My eyebrows raise. "Why?"

"Who else knows you can paint?"

I don't understand where this is going, but I won't put my friends in danger. "No one really." It's only half a lie. "My father always told me not to mention it."

"That was smart." He picks the guitar up from the sand and dusts off the base. "I'm not sure if this plan will work, but you need to show people you can paint and you need to do it now." He slips the strap of the instrument onto his back and begins to climb the rocks.

"Wait," I call after him. "How does this get me to talk with Henry?" Calder doesn't wait and I'm forced to scramble up the rocks behind him.

"Henry values creativity and intelligence, two things you don't find much of here..." His voice trails off. It's the only time I've spoken with him where he realizes the insult in his words. Maybe two things will come from my death. I'll get my answers and Calder will be a smidge better as a human being.

"Okay," I say breathlessly at the top of the cliff. The wind whips my hair around us and I struggle to tie it back. "What exactly do you propose I do?"

*

Calder's plan is too simple and he wants nothing to do with it. Thankfully, I have nothing to lose. I return to my room and unscrew my mural from the wall.

"A thing that size will draw attention," Calder explained. *"Bring it outside and into the middle of the wharf. Paint something new on it. The watchmen on duty know to report oddities like this to Henry."*

"Didn't you already report it?" I asked.

"I did." Was that shame I saw in his eyes? *"But Drake counteracted my statement saying it was nothing more than childlike scribbles."* I held my bruised hand against my chest and smiled. *Bastard.*

"Then what do I do?" The world was spinning around me, slipping from my grasp, as the ocean beat against the rocks below us.

Calder turned to look at the wall. *"After that, you just need to wait and pray."*

I don't immediately carry the mural outside. The paper that holds the likeness of my father's machine flutters to the floor. I pick it up and study the lines carefully, committing them to memory, before holding it over the flame of the whale oil lantern. It quickly disintegrates into ash and my sandals stomp out the small embers on the floor.

Paper is the most fragile object I've ever seen, but at least I got to see it before I go.

The tavern is mostly empty except for the two old men sitting at the bar.

"What is that?" Gertrude places a hand over her heart as I maneuver the large fiberglass sheet down the staircase. The bag of paints rattles clumsily against my side.

"It's called a painting. I do likenesses with color." A proud smile spreads across my face.

"It's beautiful." Gertrude leans across the bar counter to study the details closer. "I've never seen anything like it."

"I have," one of the old men mutters. His hands shake as he downs the remainder of his drink. "A long time ago I met a man who did that too. You'd best be getting rid of it, girl."

"That's the plan." I readjust my grip before carrying it out of the open tavern doors and onto the busy wharf.

It's not hard to find a gap in the rusted planks that is large enough to prop up the mural and keep it standing. The crowd parts curiously around me as they walk to whatever laborious tasks occupy their day. Honestly, I'm almost giddy as onlookers stop to admire my work. But I don't sit still to judge their reaction for long. Calder's plan was weak. Henry wants creativity or intelligence. That's fine. I'll give him both.

It's ironic that the black squid ink that started this chain of events is the very same color I choose now. Black is bold. It gets the point across and remains exactly where you place it. I stare at my beautiful paintings and then smile as I walk around them to touch the blank space on the back.

One line here, as straight as a trident reaching up from the depths of the sea, and then another. Slashes of quick strokes. This has to be methodical. It's the only way it will work.

My hand moves quickly as the memories take hold of the brush and spill themselves out onto the canvas.

"We are going to save the world," my father laughed.

"No, dad," I whisper to myself now. "But I am going to try to understand it before I die."

As soon as I've drawn the replica of the machine to scale on the length of the fiberglass sheet, I work fast to label each part I remember. This is just for me. No one who sees this will be able to read it, but maybe they'll remember it. There might be a curious child tugging on her mother's hand who will keep the image embedded in her memory. Maybe one day she'll paint it.

The feeling of triumph makes me lightheaded as I step back to examine my work. There is a crowd that has formed around me. A man stares in wonder. His jaw hangs open as he studies the paintings. An old woman gasps out loud and places a hand over her mouth. Little children inch closer and peer into my bag of paint. They watch as I smile and lift my chin proudly.

Suffocating and foreign material as black as squid ink covers my face. It blocks out the sunlight. The last image I see is of my father's machine.

*

I told myself I'd go gracefully when they came for me. I want to die with dignity. But this primitive urge for survival and fear of the unknown urges me to fight. I lash out blindly at the hands that grip me, screaming at the top of my lungs.

"I want to see Henry!" I scream, clawing at the material on my face. The hands lift me from the ground as they restrain my arms. There are so many of them. A collective silence suffocates out the sound of the sea. None of them respond to my demands. I kick out with my feet losing my sandals in the process.

One man grunts as my knee crunches against bone. I swing it again, trying to replicate the sound, but more hands clamp onto my body.

I thrash at the thousand restraints, twisting and turning, screaming and cursing them all. Something hard and heavy crashes against the side of my head. Then there is only true darkness as I slip into unconsciousness.

☦ CHAPTER NINE ☦

Muffled voices argue in the distance. It sounds like they are underwater, or maybe I'm the one underwater, but I can tell the voices belong to males. The sound is coarse and deep. I open my eyes, but I still can't see. The scratchy black material suffocates me. I want to pull it off my face. Except, my arms are bound behind my back. Struggling against the binds gets me nowhere, it just makes the whole world spin.

I can't tell if I'm lying on the cold floor of a rocking ship or if the throbbing in my head just makes it seem that way.

"I want to speak with Henry." I surprise myself at the strength of my demand. The sound of boots walking away filters through the thick black material and I'm left alone in silence. When I pull my knees to my chest, I'm able to roll into a sitting position. I instantly regret the motion as a wave of nausea overtakes me.

I force myself not to vomit into the material and lean back until I feel a solid wall behind me. My ribs hurt. Every part of me hurts. I guess it shouldn't matter when you're about to die, but it still does to me.

I take deep breaths, waiting for the dizziness to fade and try to get my bearings. I don't know why I can't hear the sea. Wherever I am must be deep below deck on the watchmen's ship where they take people before murdering them and releasing their bodies into the ocean. It isn't justice. This is murder. I'm about to die for slapping a watchman on the cheek.

"I want to talk to Henry," I call out to no one, but it gives me comfort to hear myself speak.

The whisper of a breeze dances across my bare feet. It suddenly occurs to me that I can't be below deck if I can feel the wind.

The material is yanked from my head pulling strands of my hair along with it. I flinch away from the sunlight that instantly blinds me. The sun forms a halo around a face that comes into focus. The face has a crooked nose and soft blue eyes.

"What did you want to talk to me about?" Henry asks.

I swallow hard. Now that I have what I want, I realize that I want so much more. But the plan has been set into motion and there is no arguing with the results. Henry is right here in front of me. This was my final request. I don't get another.

"What happened to my father?" My voice is shaky and hoarse.

"Your father was too smart for his own good," Henry says gently and sympathy fills his eyes. I sit up straighter and glare at him. He can keep his pity.

"What's so wrong with being smart?" Hate makes my skin crawl as I look at this vile man hiding behind a kind face.

"He didn't belong in this world." Henry smiles sadly.

"Who are you to decide who belongs here or not?" I practically spit the question. It doesn't seem possible that this man can stand here and talk to me this way.

"Because if I don't take the time to do it, then it will be worse for everyone." He shakes his head. "But this isn't what you want to ask me, is it?"

"If you already know what I want to ask, why don't you just give me the answer." I struggle to adjust my arms tied behind my back.

"You are a lot like your father," Henry chuckles. "And no. I didn't kill him and the watchmen didn't order his disappearance. By all accounts, and all the information I could gather, your father drowned."

"I don't believe you." I wish I could shut my ears so I don't have to hear his lies. "Why did you take his plans? Why did you sabotage the gear? Why did you break down his machine?"

"What gear?" Henry looks confused but his expression quickly becomes unreadable. He's a professional liar. I can see that now. He shakes his head. "Never mind that. The machine wouldn't have worked, but he made the plans for me."

"If that was the case, why didn't you just come ask for them?" I smirk.

"Because I didn't know where they were," Henry sighs. "And I didn't want to just barge into your home."

"Your watchmen had no issue breaking into my home," I huff.

"They've been reprimanded for that." Henry looks at me in earnest as if he is studying my face. "You've always stayed below the radar. I never knew you could paint. Was it your father that taught you to write letters? Can you read?"

I glare at him and don't respond. He's lying to me. This was a mistake. I should have known that I could never trust a watchman.

"If that's the way you want it to be." Henry pulls a knife from his pocket and opens it with a snap. My eyes widen in fear as I push myself against the wall behind me trying to fade into it. He moves so quickly I don't have time to react. I shut my eyes as the blade cuts into what I'm sure will be my skin.

The binding on my arms loosens and my hands are free. I open my eyes just in time to see him cut the rope that holds my feet. He grabs me by the shoulder and lifts me up to stand. I inhale sharply when I see where we are.

The wall that surrounds the earth is behind me. I can't see the ocean anymore. There is only land. The trees and plants and dirt that I remember as a child stretch out for miles all around us. But I've never been to this place before. There's a house made of stones on top of a hill. I would have remembered that. I turn to look at the wall and I can't see the gate.

"Tell me what is going on," I demand. "Is this some kind of trick? Why are we on land? You owe me a traditional burial at sea." It hits me hard that I need to see the ocean again one last time. They can't kill me here.

"You ask a lot of questions," Henry says. "You'll get your answers soon enough."

Calder comes walking over from the tree line. He looks less than pleased to see me here. The feeling is mutual.

"Now you can pester him with your questions." Henry nods.

"Sir, there has to be someone else." Calder comes to a halt in front of Henry. "Please, I'm begging you. Think of what she will say."

"What I will say?" I ask incredulously. "Since when have you ever cared what I have to say? I just want to know what the hell is going on. Am I going to disappear today?" Both men ignore me.

"That is not my problem," Henry calmly states. "You were given a direct order and you disobeyed it. Since you took this one as your project, you are responsible for it."

"I can take care of myself." I glare at the sides of their faces. "I just want to know if I'm dying today or if I'm free to go."

"Neither." Henry turns to leave. "Calder will escort you to where you need to be. I wish the both of you safe travels." He briskly walks to the trees and vanishes into the forest. My mouth hangs open, but I snap it shut when I see Calder's face burning with a mixture of anger and shame.

"You are now my prisoner," he says flatly. "We will camp in the cottage for the night and begin the journey in the morning."

"I'm not going anywhere until you tell me what is going on." I dig my heels into the soft earth. The sensation takes me by surprise. Memories of my childhood come rushing back to me. It's so different from the shifting sand. The soil feels soft and clings to my skin.

"Do I need to tie you up again?" Calder lowers his voice threateningly. "Because that can be arranged."

My heart skips a beat as I look at him. He's serious. My vision blurs. Sparks of light block out the green of the trees and the blue of the sky. Then the world begins to shake.

"Damn it," I hear Calder exclaim right before I collapse.

*

I awake inside a house. The stone walls are filled with some kind of caked on substance. It almost looks like mud. The deep brown earth I dipped my finger into and painted on rocks with. I'm lying on the softest mattress I've ever felt. Smoke drifts lazily from a black box.

Something is burning. I bolt upright and scan the small room, but there is no fire uncontained.

"You're awake." Calder lounges on a chair next to the black box of flames. He tosses a rag soaked in water to me which I almost miss. "For your head," he grunts.

"Thank you, I guess." I place the cool cloth against my forehead and it does a little to soothe the throbbing.

"You took a good hit." He nods before rising from the chair. "It should be better by tomorrow. Eat something and then get some sleep."

The moon is high in the sky and the stars play peekaboo through the tops of the trees. It's so much darker here than it is in the city. There is nothing there that blocks the light from the night and all the celestial bodies that shine down to the water.

I've lost the rest of the day laying here while Calder did gods know what. The smell of food brings a pang to my stomach. I stumble out of bed and over to the pot beside the black box. It looks like some sort of stew. I ladle it into a bowl and carry it back to the bed. It could be poison, but since I was going to die anyway then I might as well take my chances.

"What is that?" I mutter as I chew the food.

"It's rice and chicken," Calder sighs.

"The food?" I point to the bowl.

"Yes," he explains. "Rice. They grow it in the marshes. Chicken is a bird. It runs wild around here."

"Who grows it?" I swallow another spoonful.

"We do," he says softly. "The watchmen grow it."

"Why are there watchmen growing things on land?" I try to remember my time as a child here. The watchmen would bring over a cow sometimes. We got milk when we were young. Were there watchmen who stayed here to take care of the cow? I guess there would have to be.

"To help supplement the supplies we need on ship." He sits heavily onto the chair.

"Why don't you share with the people?" I lay the spoon in the bowl and study his face, wanting to see if he will tell me the truth.

"Because we don't." He stares back at me.

"I never really learned what a marshland is," I say redirecting the conversation.

"It's like a swamp." He leans back and crosses one leg over the other. "The land surrounding this island on this side of the gate is bogged down by water. It makes a good field to grow rice."

"That land is eroding," I explain to him. "It's not safe to be there."

"It amazes me how naive you people are." Calder shakes his head. "I didn't believe the stories about barbarians, but some of them were right. You need to get sleep though. Finish your food and close your eyes. No more questions tonight."

"Okay." I shrug. "Just answer my first question. What is that?" I point to the black box of fire this time so he doesn't get confused again.

"That's a wood stove." He puts his hands behind his head and his eyes close. *Wood.* I know that word.

"You burn trees?" I ask in disgust. He opens his eyes and a curious sadness creases his face.

"And you think I'm the barbarian." I wrap the blanket from the bed around my shoulders and turn to stare out the window.

*

"You're going to have to carry your own pack." Calder motions to the bag near the door. I open the flap to inspect the contents. There's food, extra clothes, water containers, and a bedroll.

"And if I refuse," I say.

"Then you starve." Calder shrugs his bag onto his shoulders and steps outside. "The shoes should fit. Pad them with extra socks if they don't."

"Hey, wait a minute." I stand inside the house. "I'm not going anywhere until you tell me exactly where it is we are going to."

"You will come with me," he states. "Either I'll tie you up and drag you the whole way or you can walk beside me. Your choice."

I hold my wrists out in front of me, challenging him to make good on his threat. "Get the rope then." He grunts and turns to stare off into the distance.

"Listen," he says. "You want answers. I'll make you a deal. One question for every mile we walk."

"How many miles are we supposed to walk?" I eye the pack on the floor skeptically.

"At least fifty."

"Fifty miles," I shriek. "How is that even possible?" The city is only five miles wide and it takes all day to get across it. I can't imagine what fifty miles looks like.

"We'll take it day by day." He adjusts the straps of the pack on his chest. "But we are wasting daylight now."

I pick up the clunky boots. "Can't I just wear sandals?"

"You need real shoes," he sighs. "Put them on so we can go."

"Will you lie to me?" My eyes fill with tears. I'm so overwhelmed with everything that is happening and I don't trust him, but I don't think I have another choice.

He studies my face and for a brief second, his features relax losing their edge of hardness. "No more lies. I promise to tell you the truth."

I breathe deeply and stop myself from crying. My feet don't fit in the boots. I dig through the pack for another pair of the itchy things called socks. It's awkward to wear the boots. They are like weights on my feet. The pack is heavy, but I manage to get it on by myself. I'm grateful I didn't lose my father's jacket in all of this because the extra padding keeps the straps of the bag from cutting into my skin.

I stand at the top of the hill and look at the rusted metal wall stretching high into the sky. Everything else I've ever owned is behind it. Everything I've ever known and everyone I love is behind it. I should be happy to have the chance to be on this side of it, but the wall divides me from my world.

"You can't go back." Calder stands beside me. "It's best to forget about it and move forward."

"Okay." The word is a whisper. I turn around so that I can no longer see it. "Which way are we going?"

*

We enter the tree line at the base of the hill. The thick branches canopy over the small path and the sun barely peeks through. I inhale deeply. The smell of rich earth and wet tree bark punctuated by crisp pine needles overwhelms my senses. It's the smell of my childhood.

If I close my eyes, I can almost hear the sound of Lena's laughter while we run away from Tordon and the other boys. A hollow ache forms in my chest as the loneliness sinks in. *I'll never see my friends again.*

Calder walks easily and quietly on the uneven terrain. My feet want to roll from side to side, but the thick boots keep my ankles steady. The trees thin out and the chain link fence that blocks the eroding land from the island appears. The fence is for the children to protect them from accidently wandering too far out and getting stuck in the swamp.

"Hang on a second," I call to Calder as he turns to follow the path outside the fence.

"What is it?" he asks.

"Privacy please." I glare at him. His cheeks flush and he turns to stare out over the swamp without another word.

I squat down behind some boulders and dip my finger in the mud. On the flat face of the rock, I quickly outline a little toy ship. It's for Zander. I'm not sure if he will ever see it, but I wanted to try to leave something for him anyway.

"Hurry up," Calder commands.

"I'm already done," I say as I walk up behind him. He continues forward without looking back.

Every few feet the path is eroded by the rising water. Twice my boots have gotten stuck in the muck and I've had to pull myself against the fence to free them. Calder walks more carefully avoiding the pitfalls without a second glance. *How many times has he walked this path?* I hate not knowing anything.

"Has it been a mile yet?" I ask in frustration.

"Yes." I can almost hear him smiling. "That was your first question and answer."

I slam my mud caked boot onto the ground, but my protest is cut short when Calder removes some reeds from the shoreline exposing a little tin boat.

"I'm not getting into that." I eye the contraption distrustfully.

"Why not?" Calder swings his pack off and sets it in the front before climbing in after it.

"Look at how short the sides are. It's going to tip over." Just looking at him in that tiny thing makes me anxious.

"It's called a Jon Boat. They are made to handle this type of water." He starts the motor with two pulls on a cord. "Get in or I'll pull you in."

I sit nervously on the little bench and unlace my boots. If I have to swim through this dirty water, I can't let these heavy things weigh me down. Calder chuckles when he sees what I am doing. He can laugh all he wants. I'm not saving him if he drowns.

The boat glides through the overgrown grasses of the marshland and winds its way through the twisting ivy hanging from rotten trees. It smells of decay here. I'm reminded of how Jillian's house smelled when Shane let the produce rot.

"I wouldn't do that," Calder warns when I get brave enough to let my fingers trail in the brown water moving past us. I glare at him in defiance just as something slimy brushes against my fingertips.

"What was that?" I ask quickly pulling my hand back into the boat.

"A water moccasin. They are poisonous," he says.

We've been traveling for what seems like an hour but it's hard to tell when I can't see the sun. The water gets clearer and the overhead trees thin out as Calder steers us around a bend. Up ahead on the shoreline are a few stone houses like the one we stayed in last night. Watchmen mill about the front yard stacking wood and carrying water.

"What is this?" I demand to know. "Why are there watchmen living here on the land in houses?"

"It's not time for a question," he says.

"The hell it's not! We've traveled at least a mile." I tighten the boots on my feet as I realize he means to dock the boat.

"You sat for seven miles to be exact." He tosses the rope to a watchman waiting on the shore. "The deal was one question for every mile you walked." I grind my teeth as Calder leaps from the boat onto shore and claps the waiting watchman on his back.

"What do we have here?" The new watchman holds his hand out for me. I refuse to take it and climb over the dinky little boat edge without any help.

"Transport," Calder says bitterly.

"Well, she's a pretty one at least." The watchman gives me a warm smile and a playful wink. "What do you do?"

I glare at him, refusing to speak.

"I'll tell you what she normally never does," Calder chuckles. "I can't ever get her to stop talking. Maybe you should travel with us. It's the first time she's been speechless." My cheeks burn as the two men laugh at the joke.

"You're both assholes." I turn and pull my pack out of the boat.

"He's only teasing." The watchman smiles. "That's how Calder is."

"Could have fooled me." I glare at Calder until the laughter fades from his eyes.

"Are you sticking around long?" the watchman asks ignoring my angry remark.

"No." Calder's voice turns hard again. "We are going to try and get as many miles in as we can before sunset."

*

The watchmen feed us lunch. They sit family style around a wooden bench table and serve what they call sandwiches. Bread is made from flour which is a wheat grown in fields. Calder excuses us before I can ask any more questions.

"It's 2000 steps a mile." He tightens the strap across his hips. "Can you count that high?"

I adjust my own pack over my shoulders trying to lift the weight up like he does. My muscles are already sore. "If an idiot like you can do it, then I'm sure I'll be able to manage. Lead the way."

It's hard to keep focus on the numbers as we travel the well-worn path up the hill and away from the watchmen's village, but I don't skip a beat. There are so many questions brewing inside of me that it physically hurts to keep my mouth shut. I need to make the first one count.

At the top of the hill the trees are sparse. A valley of thick vegetation lays beneath us and a mountain sits before us. The view is breathtaking. It goes on forever. Everywhere you look there is something new. Birds chirp and little insects bat at my eyelashes.

1999… I stop. "That's a mile. Now where are we going?" The words rush from my lips.

Calder takes another step and pauses. "That's the first question you want to ask?"

"It seems like the most obvious one." I roll my eyes.

"We are going to a community of people who live on the land." He takes another step.

"That's not a good enough answer." I hurry to catch up with him.

"It wasn't a very good question." He shrugs. I bite my lip to keep from screaming and begin to count again.

✝ CHAPTER TEN ✝

1994, 1995... A small animal scurries across the path and I make the same squeal of delight that I once did when I was a child. "There was a squirrel!"

Calder doesn't seem to notice and I've lost count of the final steps. I take another ten of them to make sure.

"Are we going to see the retirees?" The question spills breathlessly from my lips.

"No." He keeps moving forward.

"Where are we going then?" I throw my hands in the air.

"One mile. One question," he states.

"That's not fair." I stop walking. "You can't just give me yes or no responses."

"Then tailor your questions in a way that gets you the answers you want." He doesn't wait. I hesitate before following him.

*

The numbers become repetitive like a beat that matches every step. The path sharply inclines once we clear the little valley and we begin our ascent up the mountain. My legs are shaking at the end of the next mile. I stop to drink some water and foolishly drop my pack. Once my shoulders are free from the weight, I realize I never want to pick it up again. Calder stands tall as he waits for me, but a sheen of sweat glistens on the back of his neck.

"Why aren't we going to see the retirees?" I sit on the pack and wipe the excess water from my lips.

"This is as good a place as any to stop for the night." He slips his pack off his shoulders and looks around us. "I was hoping to make it further but you move slower than I'd like. This is the hardest stretch anyway. It will all be downhill after we get to the top."

"You haven't answered my question," I point out, trying not to let my relief show.

"I will," he explains. "Help me set up camp first and then I'll talk to you."

*

The sun still sets like normal here. It seems different not seeing it dip below the flat line of the horizon on the ocean, but it sinks behind the trees and night comes just the same. It's so much colder here than it is in the city.

Despite the repulsion I feel, when Calder starts a fire with dead tree branches that he scavenged from the ground I'm grateful for the warmth the earth provides. The smoke is pungent and burns my lungs. It's nothing like burning whale oil.

"Do I get my answer yet?" I'm too tired to be polite.

Calder sighs as he leans back against the fallen tree trunk. "I was hoping you wouldn't ask that one yet."

"Why?" I pull the blanket around me. It's so much thinner than tanned seal hide. I move closer to the fire.

"Because it is something that I struggle with and the answer is not an easy one." His tone is gentle. It sets me on edge.

"You promised me the truth," I say.

"I did." He nods. "How about I'll give you two questions tonight instead of this one?"

"No." I shake my head. "That's my question. I earned it."

The fire dies down casting shadows on his face and he places another fallen branch atop it. "This is one of the things you will come to understand later. I'm sure they are better at answering it than me and you are not going to like what I have to say."

"I don't like anything that is happening right now." I shiver as the flames dance higher. "Why aren't we going to see the retirees?"

"Because they aren't here." The light from the fire cast shadows on his face. "The world as you know it is a lie. There is no magical retirement community that your people go to when they get old. It's just a dream."

"I don't understand." The wind whistles through the trees sending chills across my body. "I've seen the ship pick them up. It comes every three months. My mother left on that ship."

"You've seen a ship come, but it doesn't take them to the land." Calder folds his arms over his knees and lays his head on top of them.

"Where does it take them?" My stomach hurts as it twists in knots.

"That's two questions." He raises his face and there are tears in his eyes. I couldn't care less if this makes him sad.

"Tell me." I clench my teeth and grip the blanket so hard I might rip the weak fabric.

"It doesn't take them anywhere," he whispers. "It's where they go to die."

*

Calder breathes evenly next to the glowing embers of the fire. He hasn't moved in over an hour. I lay here pretending to be asleep as the shock of what he'd said plays out on repeat in my mind. *How stupid was I to believe that a ship carries retirees to land?* But it wasn't just me that believed it. We all believed. My own mother walked onto that ship willingly.

Hundreds of people each year take the ferry from the docks out to that ship. We earned it. We've suffered outside the wall our entire lives to protect the few resources left in the world. It's our reward for doing what is right. *Was it really that long ago that all I wanted was to live on the land and paint?*

Now I've seen enough in one day here to know how foolish we all really are. In the miles we have traveled there is enough room for every family in my city to live. There is nothing around me but wilderness and the watchmen with their lies.

I fight back the bile that rises in my throat as I turn to look at Calder's sleeping form. He lays so still. I sit up making the least amount of noise possible. The pack and boots will only slow me down. *I should kill him.* There might be a knife in the bag, but I hesitate before reaching for it.

The risk is too great if he wakes up. His ancient weapon sits propped on the tree beside him. I'm not sure that I can take him in a fight, but I can quietly slip away.

I walk barefoot through the soft pine needles heading back toward the traveled path. Once I'm there, I hope the moon and stars will be bright enough to light the way back to the watchmen's little village. From there, I'm not sure how I will navigate the swamp but I'll steal a boat and figure it out as it comes.

I have to try. I need to warn everyone about the ship and the watchmen before it's too late. They need to know and we need to fight.

A branch snaps behind me and I quickly dart between the trees. It's so dark beneath the canopy overhang. *How do people live like this without the stars to guide them?* I know I'm quiet. I can barely hear myself move over the pounding of my heart in my ears.

When another branch snaps, I inwardly groan just as Calder reaches out from the shadows and wraps his arms around me.

"I hate you!" I scream. My voice echoes off the mountain and dies in the quiet of the night. I struggle to twist my body around and kick out my legs hoping to hurt him in any way I can.

"Be quiet," he whispers harshly against my ear. I lower my face to bite his arm, but he grabs me by the hair and yanks my head back before my teeth can connect with his skin.

"I said be quiet," he growls. "You're going to get yourself killed."

"Kill me then!" I scream in his face. He flips me over his shoulder and carries me back to the campsite as my fists pummel against his back.

"Hold this." He drops me to the dirt with a loud thud and hands me a stick with fire on the end. "And put your damn shoes on."

My eyes open wide as he unslings the weapon he carries and points it to the trees. Two sets of glowing eyes appear in the darkness. I hastily pull on my boots and fumble as I try to lace them.

"What are they?" I ask.

"Wolves," he says calmly.

A low growl comes from the bushes and the head of a beast appears. Its sharp white fangs reflect the light from the fire. Those teeth could snap bones. Calder fires a shot in the beast's direction and it lets out a yelp before scurrying away. The second set of eyes vanish and I let out a shaky breath. The relief doesn't last long.

Calder turns to me with his own eyes blazing. "What were you thinking? Are you trying to get yourself killed? You can't go running off barefoot in the middle of the night like some kind of savage!"

"I was thinking that I want to get as far away from you as possible." I pronounce each word as clearly as I can so they'll pierce his thick skull. "I need to go back to my people and warn them."

"Listen to me." In two long steps he's closed the distance between us and grabs me by my shoulders. "They are not your people anymore. You can never go back to them. I'm going to take you someplace better, but you can never go back to the cities on the sea. Do you hear me? You will die before you ever set foot on those wharfs again."

My lips curl into a sarcastic grimace. "Want to bet?"

Calder lets out an inarticulate growl and reaches into his bag. My hands are tied before I can fight my way out of the restraints. He laces the rope around his ankle and lays down on the ground.

"What are you doing?" I cry.

"Getting some sleep." He folds his arms over his chest and closes his eyes. "I suggest you do the same."

*

The morning comes just as I drift into my dreams. I'm standing in Meghan's kitchen. Thora is a little girl. She's almost Zander's age. Her brown hair falls in long curls down her back. I reach for her and she jerks away…

"Wake up."

Freezing cold water splashes against my face and I gasp in shock. I bolt upright and notice that the rope is gone. The spots where he tied it too tight are sore and I rub them to ease the pain.

"What makes you think I won't run again?" I glare at him.

Calder picks up his pack and grins. "You won't if you want to see where I am taking you."

*

The climb up the mountain burns my legs in ways I've never experienced. The pack rubs against my raw and bruised shoulders. I lose count of the number of steps so many times that I'm sure we've gone at least two miles. I can't think of what question to ask. I'm too tired to formulate a coherent thought and each switchback the path takes up the slope of the mountain makes me want to cry.

"Can we stop?" I break down and beg.

"Is that your question?" He arches an eyebrow.

"No." I slump against a steady tree, grateful for the support it gives. "I just need to rest for a second."

"You're doing better than I expected. The worst of it will be over soon." He says it so dismissively that I wonder if he even realizes there was a compliment in there.

"What's your question?" He sips on his water container. There are dark circles under his brown eyes making them look even darker.

"Why do the watchmen lie to us?" I ask.

"Now that is a question." He rubs his chin in thought. A stubble has formed on his jawline. It never occurred to me that he must have to shave to keep his face that smooth. Most men in the city don't shave at all.

"It's owed an answer," I say after he sits in silence for too long.

"It's probably easier to manage people when they have some type of hope." He hoists the pack onto his shoulders again. "But I didn't start the lie. It was there long before I was born. At first it didn't matter, but when I got to the cities and saw it in person, I began to question it myself. There are some things that are out of our control though."

"That's a weak answer." I grunt as I lift my pack. "If you knew it was wrong you should have tried to do something about it."

"You didn't grow up like I did." His words are soft as if he didn't mean to speak them aloud.

"Apparently I grew up a savage." I give him a smug grin. "And even I know how to do the right thing."

The next mile up the mountain is hard. It's harder than anything I've ever done in my life. The blisters on my hands from working with Aegir are miniscule compared to the ones forming in these gods-awful boots.

I struggle to breathe as we climb. Even Calder looks pale. I just want this to stop. I want the endless trudging to be over. There is absolutely nothing that I want to see over the crest of this mountain. I haven't even bothered to count steps over the past hour.

Each step is so excruciatingly slow that I'd be surprised if we've made it more than a few yards. Despite my stubborn refusal to admit it, oh gods, I want to stop walking more than I've ever wanted anything. Everything hurts and I just want to take off this stupid pack.

"We made it." Calder places his hands on his knees and takes a few deep breaths.

"Made it where?" I snap, surprising myself that I have the energy left to respond.

"To the top." He smiles. I never noticed the dimple on his dirty cheek.

"Of course we made it to the top." I climb the rocky trail as I glare at him. "Where else did you expect us to make it to?"

Calder shakes his head and grins. I don't give him the satisfaction of seeing the relief on my face, but when he drops his pack and stretches his arms, I hurry to do the same. As soon as my pack hits the earth, the wind chills my sweat soaked back. *It's freezing up here.* Calder leans breathlessly against a rock and stares past me. I turn to look at my surroundings and a heartbroken cry escapes from my lips.

I can see the ocean.

"What is it?" Calder stands up straight and surveys the area around us.

"Look at her." Pain breaks my voice into a thousand pieces.

"Look at who?" He studies my face curiously.

"The sea," I half cry, half giggle. "She is still there. She is everywhere." He turns to see the water that covers the whole world.

From this vantage point, I can see it all. The hills and valleys we crossed, the miles of swampy marshland, and the wall cutting an unnatural angle through the landscape. I can even see the outermost edge of the city where I live. It's so tiny that I can't see if the boats are in the harbor, but judging by the position of the sun in the sky, I know they'll be there soon.

Then there is the sea. The endless water stretching forever in every direction. She calls to me. I want to go back. My breath catches in my chest and tears roll down my cheeks. I miss her. I miss everyone at home. *I was so foolish and I've lost everything.*

"We have to go," Calder whispers. "Don't worry, once we descend the mountain you won't have to see this anymore."

The wind whips around us and threatens to knock me off the cliff. My tears dry on my cheeks but so many pour out that it doesn't matter. I stare at Calder trying to understand how he can leave this all behind without a second glance when it is killing me to do so.

"Why do you hate us so much?" I don't care if it's time for a question or not.

He swallows hard and looks me directly in the eyes. "I'm sorry it took me so long to figure it out, but I was taught to hate you."

"Why?" The word mixes with the wind.

"I don't know the answer to that." He smiles sadly. "But my plan is to figure it out."

The descent down the mountain is less strenuous, but there are times I'm forced to lean backwards and the weight of the pack almost causes me to slip. I don't count the steps anymore.

Instead, I focus on the colors around me. The hint of purple on a yellowed stalk growing between the silver rocks reminds me of a paintbrush. The golden-brown grass of a wind burnt clearing. The trees become thick again. The bark is deep brown, some red tinted, and in places covered with pale green moss. White trees streaked with black mix in with the evergreens. The leaves on these skinny trees are curling in a myriad of oranges and yellows. I let the sight of it all consume me, forcing out the ache of what I left behind.

"We can stop now." Calder drops his pack to the ground and massages his shoulders. I numbly remove the straps from my arms. The bag falls heavily behind me.

"You're quiet," he remarks.

"I have nothing to say." A bluebird hops on the branches above us. Its breast feathers are shockingly white, but its wings are deeply rich blue and there are little hints of grey on its head.

"Nothing?" He begins to gather wood for the fire. "Not even a question? You must have earned at least five of them by now."

"You're a jerk." The bluebird launches itself into the air and chirps indignantly as it flies away.

"Am I?" He smiles. "I thought I was being nice."

"Nice?" My jaw drops open. "You ripped me away from my family and took me away from everything I know. You lie to us and you killed both, not just one but both, of my parents. Not to mention the thousands of other retirees who lived their entire lives protecting the earth just so you and the other watchmen can burn wood!"

"Hey now." He raises his palms. "I didn't personally do any of that and I didn't rip you away. You were on the fast track to your own death. If anything, I saved your life."

"I didn't ask you to." My blood begins to boil.

"I think the correct response should be thank you." He cocks his head to the side and grins. I turn away before I pick up a rock and smash it into his skull.

"Don't go to far," he calls after me. "There are still wolves out there."

"Your stupid land sharks don't scare me," I mutter under my breath.

"What did you just call them?" He doubles over in a fit of laughter. My boots crunch loudly against the forest floor as I stomp away.

There's nowhere for me to go. I sit behind a large tree trunk and force myself to breathe. I won't cry. I'm sick of crying. I just sit and stare blankly ahead, willing myself not to think.

Darkness is beginning to fall when I hear Calder's boots moving through the woods.

"Hey." He squats down beside me. "I was only kidding."

"Go away." I glare at him.

"You need to eat something," he says gently. "Today was a hard one. I don't want you to collapse on me tomorrow."

"What does it matter?" I focus my gaze on the rotting bark of a fallen tree in front of me. Mushrooms sprout from the decay. "I'm just a savage, remember? I'm sure you people have a better use for your time. With lying to everyone outside the walls and pretending you are better than us, your schedule must be full. What does it matter if I make it to the watchmen's head quarters or wherever we are going?"

"Where do you think we are going?" He teases the question but I have no humor left in me.

"I don't know. A week ago, none of this was true." My arms hang limply at my side and my fingers slowly trail through the rich earth beneath them. "You've avoided answering this question long enough, maybe it's time you tell me."

"Will you go back to camp if I do?" He smiles again.

It's not like I know him all that well, but I've never seen this side of him and it instantly makes me defensive. "That depends on what your answer is."

Calder rocks back on his heels and sits in the dirt against the tree trunk beside me. I don't flinch when I once might have because I'm too numb to care. His shoulder brushes against mine. It's warm despite the chill of the night.

"Why don't you tell me what you think you know?" he asks. "We can start from there."

I blow hot air through my nose and fight against the compulsion to scream in his face. I'm so tired of these games. "The watchmen live in small colonies on the land while thousands of us are forced to stay on the sea. Somehow you coordinate ships to carry you around. The retiree ship is a lie, just like the training station down south is a lie. You protect the wall to keep us out so that your people can live on the land."

"So, you think the watchmen, an all-male force, has lived on the land for generations and keeps everyone else out?"

The color drains from my face and my eyes widen in fear. "Do you keep women locked up somewhere? Is this where you are taking me?"

Calder laughs. It's such a carefree sound that it eases my worries, but I'm filled with even more confusion.

"Why are you acting so weird?" I scoot away from him so that our arms are no longer touching.

"How am I acting weird?" he chuckles.

"Because ever since I met you, you've been a stuck-up asshole. Now that we are on this side of the mountain, you are suddenly sitting in the dirt and laughing." I eye him warily.

"Sorry." He shrugs. "I guess I am a little excited to be going home."

"And where is home?" I hug my knees to my chest.

"About twenty or so miles away. We can be there the day after tomorrow," he answers.

"What is home?" I roll my eyes, wishing he would just give me all the details already.

"Home is a place where a person comes from." He playfully winks.

"You are so annoying!" I scream as I jump to my feet. "Where exactly are you taking me?"

"The District of the Americas." Calder stands and brushes the dirt from his uniform. "Now come eat dinner before it gets cold."

☦ CHAPTER ELEVEN ☦

Calder's excitement grates against my nerves. But part of me wants to laugh at how ridiculous he is, especially when he pulls out his guitar and sings an upbeat tune. It's hard to merge the two versions of him together. Maybe it was just the watchman duties that turned him cold and distant.

He is still a watchman though, and I am still his captive.

I lay under the canopy of trees wishing I could see the stars as the sound of the nighttime forest vibrates around me. I miss the roaring comfort of the sea, but this too has its own sort of lullaby.

Calder snores heavily. I turn to my side and watch his face in the glow of the fire. He looks so peaceful and childlike. I sit up quietly and begin to lace my boots.

"Go back to sleep," he says and rolls to face the opposite direction. "Don't make me tie you up again."

A heavy sigh deflates my lungs and I fall back hard onto the dirt.

*

"What happened to Endre?" I ask after the first mile of the day. Calder stops whistling and silently continues to walk.

"As much as I miss your brooding and moody attitude," I call after him. "You owe me an answer."

"I'm not sure I have an answer for that one." He picks up the pace.

"You have to know something." I hurry to catch up with him. "You were the one who pulled him from the wreckage. You saw the rope around his neck."

"You saw that too?" he asks as he slows down.

"Yes, and no one bothered to mention it to Aegir." The path widens giving us enough room to walk side by side.

"I think Aegir knew," Calder says softly.

"Are you saying he had something to do with it?" I almost slap him, but restrain my arm. Hitting a watchman didn't go all that well for me last time.

"Not directly." He shakes his head. "Aegir is a smart man, but he plays a dangerous game."

"What game is that?" I ask.

"Have we walked another mile already?" He spins around dramatically, faking surprise.

"Fine," I groan in frustration. "But you never answered the original question."

"I can only speculate, but I think it was some kind of warning to Aegir," Calder sighs.

"Is he in trouble?" Worry snakes its way into the pit of my stomach.

"One step… Two steps… Three…"

"This isn't a joke," I cry. "He is my friend."

Calder pauses and really looks at me. The intensity of his stare suddenly makes me self-conscious. "Aegir is in no more trouble than he always has been." He resumes walking. "He skirts a thin line when it comes to stealing and reselling fuel sometimes. I'm assuming that this time he went a little too far. Endre must have gotten caught in the middle."

I bite my lip and watch my feet as I walk. There was so much I didn't know about the world, and now that I have these answers, I have no one to tell them to.

"Does Tordon know?" I ask after the next mile.

"I don't think he does." Calder looks straight ahead. "And I don't think Endre did either."

"Why would the watchmen kill an innocent boy?"

He glances at me from the corner of his eye.

"You don't have to answer." I cross my arms. "I already know why. The watchmen couldn't care less about an innocent boy or a boatful of the elderly. As long as you have your illusion of power then you can rule the world. My only real question is if you are happy with this whole kingdom of land you've protected? All of this, just for you. Tell me Calder, how does it feel to be a king?"

He chuckles softly and continues to walk without speaking.

"Take your time to think about it," I smirk. "It'll be my next question."

*

"I'm not a king," he states just as I count the final step of the mile. "I'm a pawn. The watchmen aren't the ones in control. We just do our job."

"Who is in control then?" I ask after the next mile.

"The council mostly. They make the decisions," he says.

The next mile takes us through a clearing. Fields of grass sway in the breeze. The sun is so much warmer without the trees providing shade.

"Why did you decide to be a watchman?" I shrug off my father's jacket and shove it into the pack.

"I didn't decide." He takes a sip of water. "No one gets a choice. All men between the ages of sixteen and twenty-two must serve as watchmen."

"Care to elaborate?" I ask. "Or do I have to walk another mile?"

He lifts his pack onto his back and turns to leave. I'm not sure if my bag has gotten lighter, but it's a bit easier to pick up. Still, my shoulders scream in agony when the straps hit the tender skin. I tighten the strap around my waist and start counting steps again.

We round the bend of a hill that is covered in thick green bushes. White flowers and clusters of purple pearls hang from the branches. I move closer to inspect them. The little bulb pops between my fingers and a sticky liquid comes out.

"Elderberries," Calder remarks looking over my shoulder.

"Can you eat…" My voice trails off. I'm not about to waste another question.

His face lights up with a boyish grin. "Did you want to ask me something?"

"I do." I leave the berries behind and continue down the path. "If they only force young men to join the watchmen, why are there older ones like Henry who still work?"

Calder chews the inside of his cheek as he walks. "I suppose there are some who like the job, and for people like that there is no place in my world," he explains. "Henry is different though. He tries to do some good."

"Killing my father is good to you?" I stop walking and glare at his back.

"I didn't say that," he sighs. "I said Henry tries to do good and he didn't kill your father."

"I don't believe him," I state.

"You are going to have to start believing at some point in your life." Calder smiles.

"That's a little hard to do when you've been lied to for this long."

*

We walk in silence for some time. I'm grateful he's stopped humming. It gives me a chance to dwell on what I've learned so far. In all honesty, I should run. To hell with this new world, I need to warn my people and let them know the truth.

But I wonder if this council Calder speaks of would listen to reason. Maybe I can convince them to change things. Then again, I can't be the only person who has ever walked this path. Wouldn't others have tried to do this? *Others*. There have been others who have come this way. Maybe there are people from my city living in this District of the Americas.

Maybe Jillian is there. The thought quickens my steps. I push down the hope that my father might still be alive. Calder seems convinced that Henry didn't lie, but what if? *No.* I can't bare the thought of losing him again. My father is dead. But maybe Jillian isn't.

"You can eat them," Calder says, pulling me from my thoughts. "The berries I mean. Just don't ever eat them raw. You have to cook them for a while first."

"Good to know." I continue walking. I lost count of the steps when my brain was spinning. To be safe, I start the recount at 1000. As we walk down yet another hill, Calder turns and walks backwards.

"I'll leave this decision to you." He smiles. I blink, waiting for him to explain himself but not wanting to fall into the trap of asking a question.

"Don't you want to ask what the decision is?" he asks playfully.

I nod, but don't speak, and have to keep my lips pressed together to hide my smile. His happiness is becoming contagious. Either that or the thought of seeing someone I know again is making me giddy.

"Fine," he laughs. "You've figured me out. Anyway, we've been making great time since you finally figured out how to walk on land. We can either push straight through and get there at midnight or make camp at dusk and get there in the early morning."

"I think I just want to get there and get this over with," I say trying to contain my newfound excitement. Another few steps and I can ask him about Jillian. Until then, I'm trying not to let hope get the best of me. "'Also, this place better have water. I could really go for a bath right about now."

Calder's face turns red and he looks to his boots. "I didn't even think about that."

"You stink too," I laugh as I push past him. "I'm surprised you hadn't noticed."

"I did," he says indignantly. "It's just that you're a…"

"Don't call me a savage again." I stop walking to stare him straight in the eyes.

"Not a savage." He puts his hands in his pockets and avoids looking at my face. "A female."

"It's not that hard to notice." My eyebrows raise. I enjoy seeing him squirm. It's another side I've yet to see.

"Of course I noticed." He shakes his head. "But I didn't think to offer you that. Forgive me. I'll make it up to you. There's a river over that ridgeline there. We can stop for a minute and let you get cleaned up. Then it's a straight shot of about five miles on the river road to the district."

"What's a river road?" I ask and instantly groan when his eyes light up. "That's not the question I wanted to ask!"

"It's a good question though," he chuckles as he continues walking. "River Road is a path directly on the other side of the bridge. We call it a road because it's wide enough for carts to travel. And you'll just have to wait till we get there to find out what a river is."

He turns to look over his shoulder. I haven't moved and clench my fist as I stand there glaring at him.

"Come on." He waves me forward with a sigh. "I'll give you a bonus question when we get there."

*

"Close your eyes," Calder instructs. I look at him like he's crazy.

"Just do it," he sighs. "I don't want you to see it until we get closer."

"How am I supposed to see where I'm going?" I ask. A smile spreads across his face.

"If you say that's my free question, I'll murder you in your sleep."

"I won't if you just close your eyes." He blocks the path in front of me.

The sun is setting above the hills. I hesitate as I look to the sky. Then I close my eyes and the colors splay across the blackness of my mind. Calder puts his hand in mine. It's rough and calloused. The warmth of it spreads across my palm. I fight the urge to release it, not wanting to stumble blindly down the path, and let him lead me instead.

I can hear water moving. The sound makes my heartrate quicken.

"Keep them closed," he reminds me. "I promise we are almost there."

A smile teases my lips and I inhale deeply expecting the sweet salty air to fill my lungs. It doesn't smell like the sea at all. My heart drops.

"You can open them now," he says.

Crystal clear blue water ripples down the middle of the earth crashing against jeweled rocks and glittering in the setting sun. I've never known the ocean to look this clear, but this isn't the ocean.

"A river is fast moving water," I state.

"It's water you can drink," he says excitedly.

I don't believe him until I kneel on the shore and scoop up a handful to sip between my fingers. "It's not salty."

Calder opens his water container and refills it. "Nope. It's fresh water."

"The sea is fresh," I exclaim.

"I'm not saying the ocean is dirty," he sighs. "It's just what they call this type of water."

"But it has to come from the sea." I crane my neck to look in either direction but I only see miles and miles of land.

"I suppose it does." He rubs his chin. "Or it at least connects with the ocean somewhere."

Upon hearing this, I quickly unlace my boots and put my bare toes in the water. It's freezing cold and tugs at my skin. The ocean is calling to me, reminding me of home. I can feel the pull of it through my veins.

"Thank you." I turn to look at Calder.

"You're welcome." He seems conflicted. "If I'd have known you could smile like that, I would have taken you to a river sooner."

I place my hand over my mouth but I can't wipe the smile away. We toss our outer clothes onto the shoreline and wade into the river. I'd be embarrassed to be this underdressed in front of him if this didn't feel so amazing.

"There's a deep pool on the other side of the bridge." He points. "It's easier to swim there, but we need to get going soon if we are going to make it home tonight."

"To your home," I say. "It's not my home."

"It's kind of your home now too." He winks. I splash at him with the freezing water just as he dives beneath the bridge.

I love the way the water pulls at my skin and dances around me, washing away the dirt of the past few days and refreshing my soul. It's not that hard to swim against the current here. It's harder to swim against the tide near the beach.

When I break the surface on the other side of the bridge, there's a deep pool surrounded by boulders. I stay afloat only long enough to catch my breath before diving back down to explore the depths. It isn't very deep. Smooth stones lay nestled against soft earth and I run my fingers across them. There's nothing as colorful here as there is on the floor of the ocean, but I guess the color in this world is outside of the river. I kick up and tread water.

"You're like a fish," Calder cups his hands over his mouth as he calls out to me. I smile up at him. "Want to see something fun?"

"Sure," I laugh. "But sitting on the rocks looks pretty boring to me."

"I haven't done this since I was a child." He begins to climb the rocks. The muscles of his back flex with each reach he makes.

"The fun is here in the water," I laugh as I wait to see what he wants to show me.

He pulls himself onto the ledge of the highest rock and turns to face me with his arms out wide. "Be down in a second." He holds his breath and jumps.

"Calder, no!" I scream, but it's a half a second too late. The water breaks and explodes a few meters in front of my face. "Oh, you stupid idiot!"

I quickly dive beneath the surface. The water is murky where the earth was disturbed and I can't see anything in it. I search and search until my lungs burn and I need to come up for air. My heart pounds in my chest as I scan the rocks calling out his name and hoping he made it out. Only the sound of the river answers me.

He's going to drown if he isn't already dead. *I could leave him here. It's my chance to run.* Cursing the gods, I fill my lungs before diving down again. I feel my way blindly across the rocks at the bottom until my hand bumps against the soft shape of a human body part. My fingers slip as I grasp at odd angles until I finally find his shoulders and wrap my arms under them. He's weightless in the water. I kick hard to get us both to the air.

The air doesn't help me. I struggle to get his body through the current, almost losing him again under the bridge. My elbows scrape against the jeweled rocks as I pull him onto the shore. Once he is out of the water, I drop to my knees in the grainy sand beside him.

I'm out of breath and my hands are shaking but adrenaline keeps me going. He still has a pulse. I turn him to the side. Water pours from his mouth, but his chest rises and falls.

"You lucky idiot," I sob against his back just as a pool of blood forms around his head.

"Oh gods." I look up to the sky wondering if they can hear me this far from the sea. Nothing miraculous happens. I'm not sure what I am waiting for.

Gently, I run my finger across his scalp. There's a gaping wound that needs to be closed. I rush to his pack and dump the contents on the ground. Then I do the same to mine. *There's no needle.* I kick the bag into the dirt, cursing everything that led me here.

"It's all your fault." I turn to Calder who lays bleeding out onto this stupid earth.

I need to do something to stop the bleeding. His thin blanket rips easily into shreds. I bind it around his head as tightly as I can. It stops the flow, but I've seen this before. If the wound doesn't get sealed shut it will continue to leak and then the rot will set in affecting the whole area. People can live without an arm, but I'm damn sure they can't live without a head.

The sun sets and the darkness reaches her tentacles across the sky. Calder is going to freeze to death if the head wound doesn't kill him first. After I put my clothes on, I struggle to get him into his uniform. I never realized how heavy he is. I give up on his boots. His feet won't fit inside them no matter how much I shove.

We need fire. He had a weird rock in his pocket that sparked when he rubbed his knife against it. I run to the trees in the distance and gather the fallen branches which I drag back to where his body lays.

This doesn't look as neat as the way he made it, but I stack the wood and dried grass in a pile and pull the fire starter from his pants. It takes me a few tries to get it to spark. It only takes a few dozen more to get the grass to catch fire.

The grass burns quickly and dies out before the flame ever touches the wood. Cursing everything, I find more dried grass and twigs. I put it beneath the wood this time. The wind picks up and I don't want the grass to blow away. The spark catches and I protect the flame from the breeze with my hand.

It continues to grow and I stare in amazement as the flames lick the wood branches. The fire cackles at me. I drag Calder by his arms closer to the heat. He's still breathing. *But for how much longer?*

I do my best to gather the discarded contents of our packs in the dark. There's food, blankets, and water. His pack holds a rope made of some material I've never touched before, an extra knife, cooking utensils, and paper with markings on it.

I bring the paper closer to the light of the fire. There are sketches of water and the mountains and trees, but it is not just a painting. It's more like a guide to what we've already seen. I hastily shove it in my pocket.

Calder's gun and guitar lay propped up against a rock. I bring them both closer to the fire. Once I have everything accounted for, I return to his sleeping body.

"You have to wake up," I whisper in his ear as I cradle his head in my lap. "I'm not sure what to do right now."

He doesn't move, but his breathing is strong. I can feel the heat of it against my leg. The fire jumps and twirls as the smoke drifts lazily to the night sky. I run my fingers through his short hair gently avoiding the wound. Paralyzing confusion drains me as I stare at the glowing orange and blues of the flames.

The moon breaks free from the clouds casting a whitish glow on the earth around us. The light brings clarity.

If I leave him on the river road thing he talked about then someone is sure to find him. With that weapon I can safely travel back the way we came. There's enough food between the two of us to last me a few days. I'll pick the elderberries and cook them like he said. I see the path easily in my mind and I think this paper will remind me of what I missed.

I'm free to go. I can return to my people and warn them.

"Wake up," I say to Calder, but he doesn't move. I need to get him across the bridge and then I can leave this craziness behind me. *I can see my sister's face again.*

The thought forces me into action. I'll figure out how to deal with the watchmen later. Right now, I need to find a way to give Calder the best chance of survival and then I can go. If I help him, we are even. I won't owe him anything.

There's a young tree where I gathered wood from. I use all my weight to break off two long branches. *This should work.* I carry them back to the fire and use the rope to tie our thick packs between them.

He's gotten heavier since I last moved him, but I'm able to lift his body up onto the makeshift stretcher. It works, by gods, it holds his weight. I grab the branches and slowly drag him across the bridge.

If I can just get him onto the road, I'll build another fire to keep him warm and then disappear into the night. The water rushes beneath us, taunting me and telling me to hurry back to the sea as I pull the stretcher over the wooden planks.

"You'll be okay." I hold my hand against his forehead. It burns under my skin. I thought it was the fire warming him. I force my concern deep down where I can't reach it.

"Your people will come for you," I promise even though I'm not sure if I'm lying. He can't hear me anyway. "Goodbye Calder."

✝ CHAPTER TWELVE ✝

You can never go back. Calder's words drift to me as a memory while I walk away. The fire I built for him burns brighter than the first. He'll be warm until someone sees him. *If someone sees him...*

The moon lights the path in front of me. I'm not scared to face the consequences he warned me of. I'll figure out a way to get back to the city. It dawns on me that I've never really been scared, not since the day I walked away from my mother. I've been confused and worried and stressed out, but scared? If I was scared, I would have stopped asking questions a long time ago.

Then why am I scared of facing the council? I stop walking on the middle of the bridge. The water rushes beneath me, telling me to go back home. Every fiber of my being wants to do as it says. *Will I even be able to reach the gate?* What if I never get the chance to warn anyone? If they stop me before I get there, what good will I have done?

Maybe I have a chance to fix all this. If I can get the council to see reason then maybe we can work together. Yes, I'm sure that others have tried. But I have something they don't. *What savage would have cared enough to save a watchman?*

I rush back across the bridge and with shaking hands load Calder onto the stretcher.

"Five miles you said." I grind my teeth as I pull him behind me down the rocky path. "You better not be lying because I'm counting every step."

*

The moon reflects off the distant fields casting shadows on rocks and trees. The shadows dance creating monsters that I focus on until they become solid shapes. I adjust the socks on my hands, wishing I would have thought to use them hours ago. The rough bark and sticky sap from the branches destroyed the skin on my palms.

I hate how slow I'm moving. Calder is unbelievably heavy. I've already had to stop and find a better branch for the stretcher when the first one broke. There is another hill up ahead. I lay the stretcher on the road and take a drink of water.

At least I can see the stars right now. Millions of them illuminating the night sky. It's the same sky I'd see standing on the pier. The same sky that Meghan and Lena can see right now.

I reach down to touch Calder's forehead. It's warmer than before and his skin has taken on a clammy sweat. He's still breathing and his heartbeat is strong, but the bandages are soaked through.

"I wish you'd wake up," I whisper to no one as I lift the stretcher and begin the steady trudge up the hill.

My arms are weak and my legs are burning. My brain screams at me to leave him here and try to find my way back home, but I don't stop. I count each step and try to ignore the pain. And with each step I'm less convinced that I can change things, but I know it isn't right to abandon him. *Even if he is a watchman.*

I let out a sigh of relief when I reach the top of the hill. The full moon glows over an open stretch of flat land. It's a beautiful sight. Giant white boulders sit at the edge of the landscape and miles of fence line zigzags through the fields. There has to be people nearby.

The downhill slope relieves some of the weight as I drag Calder along the road. A path veers off this main road. It's not as clear from the bottom of the hill, but the path seems to end at another one of those white boulders at the edge of the field.

I'm not sure if I'm supposed to turn from the road. I drop the stretcher in sheer frustration.

"Calder, wake up." I pour some water on his face. He doesn't move.

"Please," I beg. "I'm not sure which way to go."

I bite my lip as I study the fields around me. It hasn't been exactly five miles yet. I might as well just stay on this road until then and figure it out from there.

A few meters down the road, another path cuts away. It too leads to a giant white boulder. I stare at it in confusion. *Do these people worship rocks or something?*

There are steps facing me and a weird metal contraption leans against the side. The path is short so I drag Calder down it and over to the steps. The outline of a door is hidden in the shadows. It looks like some kind of dwelling. *Maybe they carve homes out of rocks.*

Excitement rushes over me. I hurry to knock against the door. Light begins to glow from the inside. My smile is so big that my cheeks ache. I raise my fist to knock again and the door creaks open away from my hand.

"What's wrong?" an old man coughs as he rubs the sleep from his eyes. He wears a white robe tied tightly around his waist. As his eyes focus on me, he suddenly turns pale. "How did you get here?"

"Do I know you?" I arch an eyebrow. I've never seen this man before in my life, but he seems to recognize me.

"Are there others?" he asks slowly as if he isn't sure I know how to speak.

"Yes," I respond just as slowly. Maybe there is something wrong with him. "That's why I stopped. I have someone who is injured. Is there a midwife or a healer I can take him to?"

"How many of there are you?" He stands on his toes and looks over my head. *I get that it's late at night, but does he not understand that someone is hurt?*

"It's just me and the injured watchman who I've dragged for miles on a makeshift stretcher," I explain. "Is there somewhere that I can take him to get help?"

The old man places a hand over his heart. "Mother!" he calls to the inside of the house. "I think you better come take a look at this."

"Is she a healer?" I ask anxiously.

"No." He waves his hand dismissively as an old woman with a matching white robe steps beside him.

"What is it Charles?" she asks the man. He points to me.

"What is happening?" She looks me over and raises her chin. "How did you get here?"

I don't mean to lose my temper, but these people are so frustrating right now. "I walked here with this jerk of a watchman who hit his stupid head and is probably dying. Then I dragged him on a stretcher for miles. Now I'm standing here, wasting time, because you people won't tell me where a healer is."

"My goodness child." Her shoulders relax. "Why didn't you just say that? Where is the watchman now?" I step aside so they can see him.

"Oh." The woman's hands flutter to her lips. "That is Mother Auburn's son. Charles, please go ready the cart. We need to get him to the hospital immediately."

"You know who he is?" I ask hopefully, willing this day to be finally over.

"I do." She gives me a warm smile. "Why don't you ride in the back of the cart with him and we'll get you both taken care of?"

The cart is just a wooden box with wheels. It's attached to the metal contraption that sits outside the home. Charles uses his feet to move us while the woman he calls mother rests against the handle bars.

The two of them changed into matching white outfits before beginning this journey. I've never seen pure white clothing. The material looks like the blanket that I wrapped around Calder. It's a wonder they don't freeze to death. I place my hand on Calder's heart. His steady pulse has slowed.

"How much longer?" I ask as the wind pushes against my face. At least this contraption moves fast.

"Just a few more minutes," the mother yells over her shoulder. "The hospital will be expecting us. I already gave them a call."

I stare dumbfounded at her back, but I don't have the time to question what she means. Charles makes a hard turn and I'm thrown against the side of the cart.

"Sorry about that, dear," the mother says. "His eyes aren't what they used to be."

Charles says nothing as he pulls the contraption to a halt in front of another giant rock dwelling. People dressed in white rush outside with a stretcher on wheels. They pull Calder's body from the cart, but I hold firmly to his hand.

"It's alright." The mother stands beside me. "They'll take good care of him."

For some reason, I can't let go. She studies my face and the universal sign of sympathy creases her eyes.

"Let her stay," she tells the newcomers.

"But Mother," one of the women protests as she looks at my clothes. The heat of shame burns my cheeks, but I still can't let go of his hand. After everything we've been through, I can't leave him alone in this foreign place. Maybe I don't want to be alone here either.

"It's quite alright," mother says. I'm so confused as to why everyone is calling her that. *How many children does she have?*

I cling tightly to Calder's hand as they wheel the stretcher inside. Bright lights blur my vision. I blink hard to bring the room into focus. It isn't a room, but a long tunnel we race down. Lanterns are in the ceiling, but they are unlike any lantern I've ever known. The light is too bright. It's like looking at the sun. Something metallic and bitter taints the air. It makes it difficult to breathe.

"We have to clean him up and inspect the wound," the rude woman in white speaks to me. "The environment needs to be sterile. Do you understand?"

I stare at her blankly. I've never met a healer or a midwife who was this cold.

"Why don't you wait out here with me?" Mother suggests, placing a warm hand on the small of my back. "I promise that as soon as he's cleaned up, you can sit beside him."

I don't want to let his hand go. He's the only tether I have to my real life in this weird world where people live in rocks and wear too much white. But they seem so urgent in their requests and this is his world after all. His fingers slip from my grasp as they wheel him into another room.

"I take it you are fond of him?" Mother asks.

"Not at all," I recoil back. "I'm just worried he won't be okay."

"Never mind that," Mother laughs softly. "This must be very overwhelming for you. Can you tell me what happened to him?"

The two versions of Calder crash against one another in my mind. There is the cold and distant watchman and the happy carefree man who was going home. I not sure what side of him he would want to show now, so I lower my face as I lie. "He slipped on a rock in the river and hit his head."

"And you saved him?" If she can see through my words, she doesn't give any sign.

"It was the right thing to do," I whisper. She pats me on the arm as she steers me to a chair.

"You'll fit in well here," she says. "Usually, you'd go straight to the welcoming center, but these are odd circumstances. I think it would be better if you wait here and see how he is doing before we take you there."

I collapse onto the chair she guides me to and rest my head against the wall. The strain of the past few hours catches up to me as the adrenaline fades. My eyes close as Mother rubs my arm. It's odd how a soothing gesture from a stranger can feel so comforting. Without meaning to, I fall asleep.

*

Hours later, the rude woman in white wakes me. "You did good," she says. "A few hours later and he wouldn't have made it."

"Where's Mother?" My voice is dry from sleep. I look at the empty chair beside me.

"Which one?" She smiles. I'm too confused to process her response.

"Can I see Calder now?" I ask.

"You sure can." Her smile grows bigger. "Let me take you to his room."

*

The room is as big as Meghan's living room. Calder lays on a bed of soft white fabric. A box on wheels flashes colorful lights and beeps. Plastic tubing runs from the box to his arms.

"What is that?" I point to the device.

"It's hard to explain," the rude woman says gently. "Basically, it is giving him water so he can heal." She glances over at my confused expression and quickly lowers her eyes.

"Why don't I give you two a minute alone?" she says as she backs out of the room. I wait for the door to fully close before rushing to Calder's side.

His pulse feels strong again and his breathing is steady. The color is returning to his face. Clean white bandages are wrapped around his head. *What is it with these people and their white material?*

I lift his warm hand up and hold it in both of mine.

"I can't wait for you to wake up so that I can make fun of you," I whisper softly. He's deep in sleep and doesn't respond. I study the lines of his hand.

A few weeks ago, it never even occurred to me that I could touch a watchman like this. Now fifty miles and a world apart later, here I am in this strange place wishing he would wake up and yell at me. The irony, or maybe it's the fatigue, makes me giggle. But the smile drops from my face when the door swings open.

A scowling woman glares at me from the doorway. "What are you doing to him?"

"Making sure that he is okay." I eye her warily. "Who exactly are you?"

She steps into the room. The harsh light illuminates her pretty features and brings out the strands of red in her graying hair. Her eyes are deep brown and familiar.

"I am Mother Morgana Auburn." She raises her chin and folds her arms over her chest. "High Mother Council Leader of the District of Americas. Now, I'll ask you one final time. What are you doing to my son?"

Dear Reader,

Can you believe that happened? I'm still in shock. She's his mother! I did not see that coming and I wrote it! You should totally leave me a review and tell me what you thought of this story. It was such a fun one to write.

And guess what? I just finished writing book three and you can find it at the link below!

The Land of Promises (*City on the Sea* series book 3)

https://www.amazon.com/gp/product/B0924Z4441

If you want to be first to know about new releases and other fun stuff, be sure to sign up for my mailing list through my website. Bonus- you'll also get a free copy of *Katrina's Story*, a short story prequel to the already published Project Dandelion Series.

www.heatherkcarson.com

Thanks for reading! If you like how I write, be sure to check out the rest of my books.

Other works by Heather Carson:

Project Dandelion (Series)

Also available on Audible!

Sent to a fallout shelter to survive a nuclear catastrophe, a group of teenagers are the last hope for humanity. Can they survive living with each other first?

Link to series page:

https://www.amazon.com/dp/B082QQ42TP

A Haunting Dystopian Tale (Trilogy)

Fawn hates traveling to the spirit realm. But breaking her indentured service contract means a fate worse than death.

"If Caraval and Grimm's Fairy Tale had a baby, it still wouldn't be as terrifyingly whimsical as this novel." - Kimberly Mearns, Owner Ink Spill Indie Book Shop

Link to series page:

https://www.amazon.com/dp/B087Q4XTQ3

Made in United States
North Haven, CT
28 July 2022